W9-CKM-290

Sparrow Hawk

Portrait of Sparrow Hawk

SPARROW HAWK

by

Meridel Le Sueur

DRAWINGS BY ROBERT DESJARLAIT
FOREWORD BY VINE DELORIA, JR.

HOLY COW! PRESS

1 9 8 7

Cover painting: *Vision of the Corn Youth*

Published in the United States by Holy Cow! Press, 5435 Old Highway 18, Stevens Point, Wisconsin 54481.

We gratefully acknowledge the assistance and encouragement of Joseph W. Grant for this project.

Library of Congress Cataloging-in-Publication Data
Le Sueur, Meridel.
Sparrow Hawk.

Summary: A white boy and his Sauk Indian friend experience changes in their frontier lives during the 1830s when the Sauk Indians under Black Hawk try to hold their lands against encroaching whites.

1. Black Hawk, Sauk chief, 1767-1838—Juvenile fiction. 2. Sauk Indians—Juvenile fiction. [1. Black Hawk, Sauk chief, 1767-1838—Fiction. 2. Sauk Indians—Fiction. 3. Indians of North America—Fiction. 4. Frontier and pioneer life—Fiction] I. DesJarlait, Robert, ill. II. Title.
PZ7.L565Sp 1987 [Fic] 87-80573
ISBN 0-930100-22-0

FOR

Bob Brown

WHO LOST HIS VILLAGE ON

THE FOX RIVER TOO

Contents

Titles of Drawings

Foreword

WRITING CHILDREN'S books is extraordinarily difficult under the best of circumstances but when the books involve a complicated story about two cultures on the cutting edge of the American frontier, the obstacles to be surmounted seem invulnerable. Meridel Le Sueur in *Sparrow Hawk* has accomplished a major writing miracle in bringing to life a story of two boys, Sparrow Hawk and Huck, who experience the joy of discovery and the tragedy of swift, mindless change on the western frontier near Davenport, Iowa and Rock Island, Illinois at the time of the Black Hawk war.

Developing Indian character in novels and short stories has a certain degree of risk in it because if one is accurate and has a solid knowledge of the Indian traditions, the temptation is to render the characters in words and dialog as nearly life as it is possible to accomplish. That worthy goal is fraught with hazards because the non-Indian world lacks the love of land, community and family that the Indian possesses at least to the degree that these things are emphasized in Indian life. And a translation of ideas and actions directly across the two cultures produces wooden Indians who grunt, groan, and talk with stilted dialog that can only be considered childish by the uninformed.

Indians really do address each other by their family

relationships and not by their given names. Thus fathers call sons, sons, mothers call daughters, daughters, and children call their parents mother and father. These kinship terms are always used because they teach us our responsibilities to the people around us. Yet when these terms appear in print, the flavor of Indian family life and respect vanish and an unintentional primitive patina appears.

The best way to correct this problem in translation is to follow the lead of Meridel Le Sueur and mix the use of family and given names according to the occasion when the major characters want to express different sentiments. By altering the flow of words ever so slightly a new mood is created and the story moves closer to the spirit in which Indians dealt with each other. Such craftsmanship cannot go without comment because it illustrates the manner in which Le Sueur viewed her writing. Words become merely sign posts for the underlying spirit of human emotions which lies at the heart of any good story. She does not try to repeat the slang of the old midwestern frontier, and rightly so, because we can only speculate about the manner in which these settlers actually talked. So again by minimizing the use of slang and inserting it sparsely into the conversations, Le Sueur gives life to an era in which common ordinary people determined the measure of history, not giants.

The wonder of this book is that it is considered

primarily a children's book and that it could have been published in the year of the Korean War when Americans were just beginning to embark on a witch hunt to ferret out the communists in their midst. The book definitely takes an Indian slant, it suggests that there are both good and bad whites and Indians, which must have been a distasteful concept at that time, and it shows the basic lawlessness of the frontier white and the helplessness of the Indian who trusted the government. Any one of these ideas, taken alone in 1950, might have been regarded as daring. The combination of ideas accurately portrays the frontier in realistic terms and tells us a considerable amount about life. Basically, Le Sueur seems to tell us, there are no winners and losers but only those people who come to understand their experiences.

The cultural purist may find a few things unsettling in this story. Sometimes a discordant note echoes such as the buffalo hunt which *seems* somewhat out of place in a setting that focuses on the Mississippi River. These allusions are proper, however, because they give us a concentrated sense of the Indian culture and because they provide a counterpoint to the story of people and corn which undergirds the narrative. Indian village life on the Mississippi was ordinary, without much excitement and not radically different than the life of white settlers in the same region. In fact it is the ordinariness of life, the relentless movement of a new civilization across an ancient land that needs dramatic counterpoint in the occasional glimpses into Indian life as it was traditionally lived.

On the whole, Le Sueur provides a serious look at some old and familiar questions in a manner that should please her young readers and provide them with food for thought about the nature of the life journey they are undertaking. One cannot ask a writer to do more and one should not expect less.

—Vine Deloria, Jr.

Sparrow Hawk

SONG OF *A Young Warrior*

SPARROW HAWK was riding with the hunters. They had made a surround of a herd of buffalo and now the hunters thundered over the prairie, yelling, shooting their sharp arrows into the bright air. Sparrow Hawk was going along to shoot calves. The chief of the tribe, Black Hawk, rode beside him rearing on his splendid horse, the arrows flying from his bow in quick flight. Then suddenly Sparrow Hawk saw that Black Hawk's horse, on the outside of the thundering buffalo was pushing his own horse Treads-the-Earth, inward toward the surrounded buffalo, straight toward the running flanks of a great bull. Other riders closed in and he could see that he was being crowded alongside the bull so that his own horse screamed and he thought he would be carried away, but Black Hawk pressed close upon him and his face seemed to say what he always said around the campfire: "You are old enough to overtake the buffalo and we shall see whether you are strong enough to drive the arrow in. Do not be afraid; ride your horse close and let fly the arrow with full force. If the buffalo turns to fight, your horse will take you away but above all things, do not be afraid!"

And he was afraid. He felt he was not strong enough to drive the arrow in but he had no choice with his hero, Black Hawk, riding close and his long, sharp face driving him. He drew the arrow, let it fly, and as his horse plunged ahead he saw it drive into the animal, clear to the feathers of the arrow, then sheer off, and looking back he saw blood coming from the bull's mouth. Suddenly he let out a great yell, for he felt he had done something great.

The herd that had not been felled ran on into the valley. The Indians reared their horses back to the animals they had killed, and Sparrow Hawk, sitting his horse in a way he had never done before and trying not to look as big as he felt, rode back to his bull that lay on the prairie grass. Black Hawk looked down from his horse, smiling. "You did well. Your lodge will never lack food."

Sparrow Hawk felt his mind big for what he had done. Being the only child, he had to provide the meat and corn for his mother, Evening Star, since his father had been killed by the Sioux. For the first time he leaned over his own bull, cut the meat, hung it from the hips of Treads-the-Earth, and trying not to smile with pride, rode back with the warriors into the Indian city of Saukenuk.

He felt himself shaken as if someone had grabbed him from behind. He turned to fight and heard his mother cry his name and he woke, and knew that he had dreamed again for the hundredth time, of his first great hunt only a month ago, when he had killed the big bull buffalo and brought the meat to his mother's lodge.

His mother, Evening Star, laughed, "You have been fighting and crying in your sleep."

"I was dreaming of my first buffalo. I did kill that great buffalo? I did bring the meat to your lodge?"

"Yes, my son. You take your father's place."

"Where is the deerskin bag of corn I must take this day to my white friend Huck? Is it safe? There are many enemies."

"It is safe," the mother said, "And you must be many-eyed to see your enemies."

They finished their breakfast and Sparrow Hawk could hear the boys splashing in the Rock River which would be harvest cold, and where the fishes came up to the shallow water so you could catch them with your hands.

Buffalo Dream

"Black Hawk did not return during the night," Evening Star said, "I pray he has a vision on the hill that will save our nation, our land, our corn."

"Black Hawk will never desert his people like Keokuk," Sparrow Hawk said. "He will return for the Corn Dance tonight, for the Warriors' Dance. Maybe he will even come down for the La Crosse game this afternoon between the Yellows and the Whites."

"Be careful, this day, my son," his mother said, "there are many enemies for your cache of corn."

"I will be careful," he said, "I will take the deerskin bag and go to Huck's." Huck was his white friend. "I will stop at the field in the bottom lands where I have not taken the seed from our prize corn yet."

"There are many enemies," she said. "There are the white soldiers now on our Rock Island where we used to go when you were a baby and the days were all shining with peace and the air without arrows. There are the 'friendlies,' our own people, who are ready to betray us. There is the evil son of Keokuk, Struts-by-Night, who, like his father, betrays us to the white traders, splitting our nation, and there are the bad Vandruff boys and the worst is Shut-One-Eye who would kill you if he could. Enemies as thick as arrows."

"When Black Hawk comes all my medicine will be good, all will be strength, courage and luck."

Sparrow Hawk went out in the cool September sunshine and wondered if Black Hawk had his vision in the hills, of courage, of fleetness, of some way to save their nation from being split, from losing the lands upon which they had lived for hundreds of years.

The lodges were stirring and the younger boys bathing in the stream now turning cold in the night of the falling leaves. He ran down beneath the great elms, past the heaps of golden corn that had been brought in from the fields yesterday. Already the women sat at their pestles grinding the corn into meal for the winter lodges. He ran past the birth lodges past the great square where games and dances were held and down where the Rock River joined the Mississippi and where his people, the Sauk, had built the greatest city in the West, with permanent bark lodges, streets and alleys, and the public square, where already the old men practiced on their drums and pipes and their glib tongues for storytelling in the Corn festival of that night.

He did not forget to look for his enemies. Since they had come back in the spring and found the Vandruffs in Black Hawk's lodge and fences built around the old corn lands, and squatters living in their wooden houses, you had to look all ways for enemies so it would have been good to have had three heads, or even four to look all the ways of the compass.

Cold chills came on his neck and it wasn't the cold morning. He knew he was being watched. Keokuk would like to know where Black Hawk waited the vision, or the Vandruffs would like to know what was in the deerskin bag, or where he and Huck had their corn cache for the winter but they could pluck his legs off like an old grasshopper before they would find anything out from him. Everything depended upon the corn he and his white friend Huck had grown and they would never destroy that.

Struts-by-Night, taller than he, with a dark evil face, barred his way from the yelling boys in the river. The little boys and even the fishes seemed to be watching. Sparrow Hawk tried to say to himself his courage song, but it stuck in his throat like a fishbone. Why was Struts-by-Night so tall? But he looked up and held the narrow snakes' eyes of his enemy, Struts-by-Night, who gave him a push with his hand. "Big Buffalo hunter," he sneered, "Big Sparrow Hawk now and where is your great chief Black Hawk? Run away like a rabbit! You better follow my father Keokuk. He has big white medicine now, smokes with the white chiefs."

"Traitor Keokuk!" Sparrow Hawk said, afraid of his own voice but standing up straight. The other boys had gathered round now and a yell went up. Sparrow Hawk went on, "Black Hawk remembers his fathers. He remembers the good of his people—not only to dress himself up like a white grandfather in Washington."

"Yah! Yah!" yelled the boys on his side.

"Hey! Hey!" yelled the boys on Struts-by-Night's side and they began to push each other.

Struts-by-Night said, "The white man is rich. He can give the Indian much if we do as he says."

"If we become slaves," Sparrow Hawk cried, "it is better to die fighting. . . . We did not become a great nation of men and warriors to give away our honor and our lands. Black Hawk will not bargain our land away for cheap medals and pieces of papers and the betrayal of the slit tongue traders."

"Yah! Yah!" both sides cried, "Hey! Hey!" and they all began to hit and push each other. Sparrow Hawk gave a push to Struts-by-Night, and his enemy seemed to melt away and without looking, trembling at his strange success, he walked to the river, turned and yelled, "We'll beat you into the ground at La Crosse this afternoon. Last one in the water is a rabbit!"

There was a shouting and a splashing as they all jumped into the water, splashing, churning like the white man's fireboat, that sometimes came into the shallows of the islands of the Rock River.

Lo, Sparrow Hawk, he am I
the corn youth!
the corn youth!
the corn youth!
He am I. Sparrow Hawk.
He am I.

Sparrow Hawk sang as he looked over his La Crosse sticks for the game against the Yellows that afternoon.

Evening Star, was stringing squash pieces to hang for drying and she said, "With the Hawk for totem you have much to live for and this winter when you are the hunter for our lodge I want you to wear your father's big cap, made of buffalo skins, with the fur ears on the side stuffed with antelope hair so they stand up like a jack's ears and give you fleetness, and when you look over the dry grass of a hill for game you will look like a peaceful rabbit!"

"My father's big cap!" Sparrow Hawk remembered the cap hanging on the pole of the lodge drying, remembered when it covered his whole face and his father would cry, "Hey hey! Look at my little warrior!" and he remembered his father, a big warrior telling him before he had gone to fight the Sioux in the winter, "My only son, to be brave is what makes a man. When older people speak to you listen. When you are to go and drive the horses, go at once, do not wait. Get up early in the morning. Take good care of your weapons. Be in front of the fighting. Defend your people. Strike hard at the enemy. Say to yourself, I will be brave. I will fear nothing. If you do anything great do not talk of it. Do great things and others will see it soon enough. Let your comrades speak of your brave acts. The people will then look upon you as a man. Do not let the wind blow my words away."

He put on the big cap of his father, "Now I am a hunter," and he began to sing:

Lo, Sparrow Hawk, the flint youth am I,
He am I.
Let my enemies shake like leaves
Let them run like rabbits,
Let them hide like owls in winter,
The flint youth am I
He am I!

His mother smiled, "You are a vision hunter, my big son. This is the best kind of hunter."

"He doesn't always bring home the bear and the deer and the buffalo," Sparrow Hawk said. "Sometimes he is out with his friend Huck looking after the prize corn!"

"The corn feeds us. The big corn you and Huck have grown may make peace between the Indians and the white people. It is a dream of corn. Without dreams, the great Manitou says, men will starve."

"Black Hawk says this too. It is so. What do you wrap in the sack, Mother?"

"It is your father's deer suit."

"Let me have it now!"

"Hah, you would not fill it now. When you ride with the warriors to war you will wear it. You come from a people, brave always, before the seen enemies, and before the unseen enemies. Never show fear upon your face."

He wished he could wear his father's big cap for this day he was afraid. He would have to ride through the

Fort full of white soldiers. He would have to get the corn from the bottom-land fields when Shut-One-Eye would be waiting to claim it for his own. He would have to take the deerskin of the best corn to Huck's house across the island where Struts-by-Night would be waiting with his gang to steal the corn they had grown together for three years until they had made the cobs full of corn as they had never been before. He and Huck would have to take the deerskin bag full of the best corn to the cache below the Fort in the cave where the Great Spirit in the form of a giant bird used to live. Here they would hide the corn safe for next year's planting. For Huck and Sparrow Hawk both thought that if they could raise more corn the great White father in Washington would let them stay on their land and grow corn for the middle west Forts, where many white soldiers had to be fed, and who also liked the whiskey made from corn and the fat pork of the country pigs fattened on corn.

He had the vision from his father who had fought with Black Hawk in many wars, had sat in the councils of the Five Nations, and had been killed in the battle of the Sioux, that with corn enough for all there would be no wars. The Sioux were an enemy because, hunting the buffalo, they raised no corn and came in bad years to steal the corn caches of the Sauks and the Winnebagoes. With corn enough for all, big caches to trade for meat and silver and salt, the fathers would not be killed so often.

So this day he must win in the La Crosse game against his enemies. Black Hawk must come down to the council fires so Keokuk would not, with his silver tongue, rule the people, and he must get the corn together that he and Huck had raised for the spring cache. And there were many enemies, standing in the day, to attack him and he was a young boy, even though he had killed his first bull buffalo, and he was afraid.

The Kind Corn

HIS HORSE, Treads-the-Earth, was waiting for him in the pasture. His mother watched from the lodge door fearful of his enemies. "Be many-headed," she had said, "many-eyed. They come from all directions."

He sat straight on his pony and let its slow rocking in the warming sun make a song in him, till gradually the corn song killed the fear a little and even Treads-the-Earth jogged along happily:

The corn grows for me
the corn youth!
the corn youth!
Many kernels grow for me
Sparrow Hawk.
He am I!

He could make as many songs as he had dreams, singing the first line, repeating it, letting it grow into a song. To the slow jog of the little horse he began the words over and over—"Let the people have corn! Let the thunder from me flash! Let the basket bearers come. Let the corn maidens put down their hair. Let the kind corn grow!"

For he was singing about the new corn in the deerskin bag around the pony's neck, of the long journey of his white friend, Huck, to the village to bring the corn, of how they had made many kernels grow on the cob, two where there had been one. He thought next year they would triple the corn and make possible the dream of the Sauk and the nations of the East, led by Tecumseh, of a great United Nations of Indians, dwelling on their own lands in peace with the white nations, with corn enough for all.

He had to remember to make songs that would be bad medicine for his enemies too. So he sang:

Lo, Sparrow Hawk, the flint youth am I.
Let my enemies shake like leaves,
Let them run like rabbits,
Let them hide like owls in winter,
The flint youth am I
He am I.

He would think then of the arrows he would make, short and sharp, for the enemies of the Sauk.

His enemies were also the enemies of his white friend, Huck. Now the tribe of the Sauk were not only menaced from the whites without, but from within by the split of Keokuk, who had divided the nation and wanted his followers to leave Saukenuk, give it to the white man, and never return. Those who followed Black Hawk said that the treaty paper, signed in St. Louis by three men full of firewater, was no good, that land could not be signed away by any man, that it belonged to the Great Manitou and was for men to use, never to sell.

Struts-by-Night was the son of this vain Keokuk and they both strutted about in white man's clothes, riding fine horses, wearing many medals, and rich with money and gifts. Struts-by-Night even wore a hat like the enemy.

But the corn songs were the best. Corn had been rich in the life of Sparrow Hawk. When he was a baby he was hung in the spring sun so the birds lit on his head, and he heard the women singing to the corn seeds and the singing of the young girls in the corn dance. Older, he had sung himself, helping his mother dig the holes and drop the corn kernels in, four to a hill and pat it over with his hand, singing lullabies for the baby corn. His mother had told him you cared for corn as for a child and evil was the one who destroyed it or lost a grain. His mother said when you reaped the field sometimes you heard a small cry and going back in the field you found a cob of

Portrait of Keokuk

corn crying, "Don't leave me. Don't leave me." You had to sing to the corn as to a child while it was growing or it would be unhappy. It liked to have the girls singing from the field platforms built above the fields for watchers and singers. For corn had enemies also that you had to fight. There were crows and magpies, gophers and bad boys. You had to put up a scarecrow and the younger children sat on the raised platforms and watched, making loud songs to scare off the birds. Sometimes a tree was left in the field for the watchers. All through the moon of the cherries you had to watch.

Then came the Juneberry season and then the chokecherry season. Then the corn married in the hot sun and the pollen fell upon the long silk threads and the corn grew fat in the green sheath, and ripened in the hot days and you sang another song for the ripening. Then the women put their thumbnails into one stripped cob and if the milk flowed it was time for the harvesting. The big buffalo meat kettles were scoured for the feasting and the young men came to the field with grass plumes in their hair and the young girls, their hair oiled, came in their fine dresses, and hoof bangles and elks' teeth chains. They would all be yelling and singing, the young men on one side of the field, the young girls on the other, bearing to the center, stripping the big, fine ears, saving the best for seed, stripping down the husks. The finest ears were braided and hung, ten to a pony. The smaller ears went into the baskets and for days the women crushed the kernels with crushing stones and dried other cobs on the corn stage before threshing.

For three years now he and Huck had tried to make bigger ears of corn so the winter caches would never be empty and the deep winters never bring famine. The pony jogged along as Sparrow Hawk sang:

Ho, the corn youth am I!
He am I!

The Indians guarded the field day and night where the prize corn had come to ripeness. The marked stalks stood hidden with the others, but suppose the Vandruff boys had come in the night and driven off the Sauk boys and beaten down the best corn and taken it for the Vandruff whiskey stills? Shut-One-Eye would stop at nothing. He was called that because when he saw anything he wanted he shut one of his little pig's eyes and took it. He was one of five sons of the Dutchman, Vandruff, who had taken the Sauk land the last winter while the Sauks had been off on their winter hunt. Now they claimed the ancient Indian lands for their own, had built fences, drove over with their oxen and plowed with the awful wooden plows of the white man.

Black Hawk had refused to fight them for he wished for peace and did not want to provoke war.

Sitting his horse on the bluff above the river bottoms, Sparrow Hawk saw that Keokuk's lands had been husked the day before and the corn still stood in golden piles, and now the familiar women and children, followers of Keokuk, would gather the corn for their final journey across the river to Ioway, and they would not return in the spring with the followers of Black Hawk.

Turning his horse down the path to the rich bottom lands, fearful to see the field lying flat and ruined; he thought, "could a nation cease to exist, the memories of a people lost, the City of the Dead, where my father lies, lost to them forever?"

Holding his breath he turned out of the thicket and there stood the field of green, many-fingered corn, folded into the wind and light, gleaming like green waves. On the platforms sat the boys guarding the field, playing some bone game, while the magpies chattered above them, flashing like blowing paper in the corn sun.

He left Treads-the-Earth nibbling some of the fat green, and to fool the gaming boys slid down the dark green tunnels of corn, looking for the marked stalks of the corn planted late to withstand the frost. He took hold of the fat green cobs and as he pulled down the moist sheath he was delighted to see the cob full from end to end, and plucking off one of the fat kernels he tasted the sweet, white milk. Never had he tasted anything like it. He looked with delight at the fattest, milkiest grains of corn, jutting milk where he broke the skin with his nail or teeth. He plucked all the ears, and swiftly running, crouching down below in the corn, dark as in an underground sea, he darted from stalk to stalk that he and Huck had marked. He braided the ears together and slung them over his shoulders.

Then he heard Treads-the-Earth neigh sharply and the little boys cried out. Crouching, he ran to the end of the tunnel where the pony still stood; his lips back over his teeth, as he shook his head saying—"Hurry—hurry." He leaped to the bare back and the pony skirted the corn field, and looking back he saw the Vandruff boys spurring their ponies around the field, shooting their guns into the air wildly. The little boys crouched under the platform and the magpies and crows screamed into the thicket.

Treads-the-Earth straightened out as they entered the thicket and Sparrow Hawk lay along the pony's back, hugging the fragrant braided corn. He let her follow the trail she knew, doubled back, and started toward the island where the Fort stood, through which he would have to ride to reach the farm of his white friend, Huck.

Now Sparrow Hawk felt like shouting. He was no longer afraid to go past the store of Colonel Davenport, the fat jolly storekeeper, who always wanted him to come and work there and learn the ways of the white men, and how to play cards, and laugh, and joke. The good sweet corn swung in a song of its own over the back of Treads-the-Earth and Sparrow Hawk got many things into his song—the glorious history of his nation; how they had built the great city of Saukenuk, the greatest city then in 1832, west of the mountains and the most beautiful, a city of elm bark lodges, laid in long streets and alleys, all coming together in a square where the youth learned the National dances and the ancient songs, taught by the old men and the seasoned warriors.

The city stood at the mouth of two great rivers, the Rock and the Mississippi, and drained a fertile valley, the rich water coming from a plateau of three thousand miles where the peaceful nations of the Menominee, Winnebago, the Sauk and the Fox had lived as farmers, hunters, and fur traders for centuries. They left their city unguarded, for no enemies would come while they were away. They went north after the corn harvest to hunt meat and fur-bearing animals and came back to their ancient corn hills in the spring.

Sparrow Hawk stopped his pony to hear the ancient music of the Rock rapids as they purled around the Rock Island where now the white man had built a Fort. This had been a sacred place of the Good Spirit who lived in the cave below, who had the shape of a great bird with wings the span of eight horses. But since the bluecoats had come—or the Long Knives, as some called them, or as the little boys yelled after them, "the men with hats," —since the Fort had been built with the guns pointing

Saukenuk View

to the city of Saukenuk, a terrible thing had come into the singing of the Sauk, an awful fear that what had happened to the Indians of the East would now happen to them; that never again would the Council fires of a free nation burn; never again would he visit the grave of his father in Chippionoc, the silent City of the Dead.

And now again in the Corn Moon the White Father said, "Move—depart—cross the great river never to return, leave the Signal Towers where the fires flash news to all the valley; leave the dead and the kind corn and the deer and the buffalo trails; leave the house of your birth and the tall elms arching over the home village, and the smoke fires in the evening, and the women at the corn kettles singing at harvest. Leave forever the day of the Crane dance and the day of the dance of past Courage when history was told, and now the day of the loss of all the dear and familiar things that make a place home."

The pony blew through his lips and backed away and Sparrow Hawk saw far down at the river's brink, a sentry. He pulled the pony back. He would take the steep path across the river to the island. He could see another sentry on the island which in his youth had been the place where the children swam and picnicked. Below in the great cave, there was darkness now and the sounds of empty water for the Great Spirit had fled. Here they would hide the cache of corn for spring planting.

The sentry took off his hat and wet the inside of it and Sparrow Hawk, not wanting to spoil the good medicine of his corn news by meeting an enemy, turned his pony down a steep, pathless decline. The sentry shouted to the one on the island. He heard the click of their guns and their clumsy feet through the underbrush. He let the horse enter the water, drift down until he came to a white sanded beach and silently he let Treads-the-Earth gain the sand and without a sound, moved up a hidden path onto the plateau, leaving the sentries threshing the brush on the steep declines, shouting to each other in the foolish way white men did in the forest.

In the deerskin bag, hanging with his trophies—a deer's ear for swift hearing, an antelope foot for swiftness—was the new corn, more fertile than any other, and he and his white friend would sing together a mighty song.

Flint Youth

Before he got to the Fort he heard a shot. Dismounting, he crept to a thicket that edged the plateau of the island. Through the hazel thicket he saw Standing-Bear, a young warrior, leaning against a tree holding his useless arm from which a steady stream of blood flowed down his buckskin pants. Opposite him with a smoking gun stood Shut-One-Eye, laughing and shouting insults. Silently Sparrow Hawk fit his arrow into the bow, there was a soft wang, and the arrow pinned Shut-One-Eye to the tree behind him and he stood yelling and pulling at the fringes of his coat.

The two sentries who had been looking for him, hearing the shot, ran into the clearing in the thicket. Others came running from the Fort. Sparrow Hawk turned to run, but he felt himself tackled from behind and he was being held and beaten. He remembered Black

Hawk's warning, "Do not lift a hand against the white man, it will make an excuse for an attack." So he gritted his teeth and did not even cry out. Then to his surprise he saw his attackers fly through the air, and someone was lifting him from the ground and he saw under the yellow shock of uncombed hair, like grass, the freckled grinning face of his friend, Huck. He was using some very bad language too and a blue-coated soldier was jibing at him, "I told you not to pal around with an Indian," he said. "You folks are good people but you'll get into trouble with Indians. The only good Indian is a dead Indian."

"He's my friend," Huck said.

The bluecoats were running from the Fort anxious for trouble.

"If'n you like your hide, Injun," one of them said, "you'd better stay off Fort grounds."

"Says you," Huck said. He was a tall thin boy but quick as a cat, and wiry and strong. "Sparrow Hawk here is a friend of Colonel Davy's and he says to come to the Fort any time. He wants him to work in the store even."

"Colonel Davy wants to see me," Sparrow Hawk said. "He wants to see my new corn."

"So yore makin' corn. Take a little swig of this, Injun. Nothin' like a Indian with a little fire juice in him," said one.

"I don't drink it," Sparrow Hawk said.

"You'll drink this and like it," said the soldier as he grabbed him, trying to force it down his throat, when

The Corn Youths

Huck tripped one of them and the others went down with them in a drunken tangle. The other soldiers, easily amused, all laughed and one of them said, "What do you want for that beaded belt?"

"I made it. It is my totem. Nothing could buy it," Sparrow Hawk said.

"You can buy anything from an Indian. I'll give you this looking glass for it."

"He doesn't want to sell it," Huck said.

Sparrow Hawk said, "I don't want to sell it. I do not care for selling. We did not sell the land and now the white man says we did."

"You bet you did," yelled one of the bluecoats, "and you took our goods for it."

"Old shoes and looking glasses and beads—what is that for the land of our fathers and the great nation of our people? This is the Sauk nation, a great and honorable people."

"There is only one nation," said a soldier, "the American nation."

"There is the Sauk nation too."

"Well, there won't be. We'll rub it out like I could rub you out standing there and it would be just as legal as hunting."

"What is rub out?" Sparrow Hawk asked Huck.

"We will go," Huck said. "We are going to show some corn to Colonel Davy. We have done nothing wrong that I know of."

"Don't you want to sell the belt?" said a soldier taking hold of Sparrow Hawk. "Take a drink and you'll want to sell anything."

"He told you he don't want a drink," said Huck.

"That's right," said another soldier. "This is a free country, free and equal, remember that."

"That didn't include no red skin," another said.

"It did until we wanted their land," said the good soldier. "Then they become Lo—"

"Lo—who," shouted someone.

"Lo, the poor Indian," and they all laughed and the soldier tried to grab the belt, but Sparrow Hawk whirled away and kicked him in the shin, the way Huck had taught him to fight the white man's way, and the soldier began hopping on one leg and howling so loud that the others laughed. Huck and Sparrow Hawk saw Standing-Bear running down the path, and they turned and ran back to the pony. They both mounted, sitting sideways on her, and looking into the green sheaths of the corn.

The boys rode in silence. Sparrow Hawk was ashamed for himself and for his friend Huck. "I know," he said, "all white people are not alike. The same traders who want our land want yours. What's the prayer to your Manitou you are always saying?"

Huck sat sideways on Treads-the-Earth, his long legs hanging almost to the ground. He always grinned and said, "My feet touch the ground too late." Now his face was long and solemn, "All men are created equal, we say on our paper."

"We have so many things alike. My nation believes the people are the only power of our nation."

"We have so many things alike," Huck said. "Then something like this happens. Some men signed a paper for this land, paid much money for it."

"And the big guns are pointed at us, and the men want to shoot them very bad. It seems no use now."

"It's always some use," Huck cried. "Why look at this corn. There has never been corn like this. We have made something together that will feed people. Remember how I showed you in the book the way corn grew from a tiny grass bending in the wind, way down in South America and maybe in hundreds, and thousands of years people like us, of every nationality, made grain by grain, made the cob thicken to hold it, made the seed grow larger? Remember? They started out scratching the earth with a jaw bone. Remember? They'd get a couple of ears with more grain and they'd save those. Remember? Pretty soon they had enough to save to grind for winter so they didn't have to go hunting, they could have more kids, bake bread, make stuff. The corn began to travel north. Remember?"

"I remember," smiled Sparrow Hawk at his friend. "Our old men tell about how a beautiful woman was seen by two of our ancestors when they were out hunting.

She came down from a corn-blossom cloud and thinking she was hungry, they took her some roasted deer. She told them to come back in a year to the same spot and they would find a gift for their generosity. In a year they came back and they found that where she had been sitting tobacco grew, where her right hand had touched the earth the corn grew, and where her left hand had touched grew beans."

As they jogged along, Sparrow Hawk told how they made offerings to the earth mother so she would bring forth strong plants, to father rain to care for the young green corn god, and offerings to the boy, Pollen, and the Corn Maiden within the corn, whose mating brought forth the seed. He told how they danced at corn planting and at harvest, as they would dance this night to celebrate the new corn the Indian and white boy had made together, breeding the corn, stalk by stalk, culling the best ears, saving the corn, keeping the pollen from blowing in the wind.

"Now," said Huck, chewing on the sweet corn, "if the white kernels of the corn thought they were better than the red ones the corn would be bad." They put their arms around each other and began to sing low like bees so their enemies would not hear. The Vandruff boys and the soldiers could be heard a long way off. Struts-by-Night would attack in the woods. Animals would watch them go by.

"Look," pointed Sparrow Hawk, "the deer has been

Vision of the Corn Maiden

feeding here. See, the plant is broken off. He is walking slowly, not frightened."

"How can you tell he was not frightened?" Huck asked, always amazed at the Indians who read the earth like he read a book.

"Because he is wandering back and forth, flower to flower. He did not see or smell any enemies."

It was in this way that the red and white boys and girls became deep friends, played together at the Fort or at Saukenuk, sometimes Indian games like La Crosse or American games like run-sheep-run or tag, and the children loved each other as brothers, and there was much knowledge between them that they gave to each other.

Sparrow Hawk had taught Huck all the things he had learned: how to go on the hunt and live days without food or water; how to split a tree branch, set a stone ax-head into it, let the tree grow around it and then cut it down for an ax. He taught him how to get through the woods noiseless as smoke; how to hunt animals down wind so they will not smell you; how to trail the moose, the buffalo, the bear, wolf, beaver, raccoon and every kind of bird. He taught him how to make warm winter clothes from the rabbit and how to sew with rabbit sinew and make needles and fishhooks from rabbit teeth; how to gather herbs in the spring when the strength is in the roots; in the summer when it is in the flower; and in the fall in the seed; and then in winter when it returns to the roots; about herbs for healing—the moccasin flower and the skunk cabbage for hysterics, the spicewood for fever, tansy and burdock and healing teas of sarsaparilla and mullein, of milkweed and spiderwort and wild spikenard; and how fern seed was a medicine for peace.

Huck taught Sparrow Hawk the Word in the book and how to understand what was being said at Colonel Davy's store until one day Huck had cried, "Why, you speak like a native," and then in astonishment had rolled over in the corn field and yelped, "By hickory, you *are* a native!"

"I think someone is following us," Sparrow Hawk said, "Keep your neck stiff."

"Who you think it is? We'll head into the Fort and go past Colonel Davy's store and they won't darst to touch us. Keep talkin'."

"They won't think it's corn we got in the bag," Sparrow Hawk said. "They might think it's gold. But nobody seems to think that corn is wealth. Someday corn will be the wealth of this nation."

"We'll have a corn democracy," Huck said, waving his arms the way he did when he got excited and scratching himself all over as if an idea was something like a flea, who jumped from his head to his arm, to the seat of his breeches, wriggled up his spine and entered the great thicket of his grassy head. "Corn is for everybody. Anybody can raise it. You can carry corn over a big space. Women can plant and hoe and reap and the man can do somethin' else. You're independent. It's your food, money, it's hogs, fat babies."

"Corn is like land," Sparrow Hawk said. "It belongs to all. The Great Spirit gave it to his children to live upon and raise corn. It belongs to the person who uses it and makes things grow. All red men have equal rights to land and corn."

"You see both our nations got corn democracy. Some hogs want all the land and corn, they want to root everybody out of the trough. Sometimes you got to do away with a hog that makes all the rest thin and wild."

"Let's go to the plateau edge there and look over the valley," Sparrow Hawk said, "and see who is following us. The white people think because they can't see you, you must not be around. This has caused their death. They go in the valleys and along the level roads because it is easier and every rabbit can see them."

They crawled to the top of the rolling hill and lay on top in the sun looking over the prairie a long, long way. Across the Rock River they could see a dark herd of antelope and six elk walk to the river's brink on the island to drink. Everything was quiet; the animals they could see seemed not to be moving, to be standing in a shadowless noon. The birds were not in the air and there was no smoke. The cranes were silent or had flown, the magpies did not fly to and fro, waiting for the death of a buffalo, or for people to fight and kill each other so they might feed on the flesh.

"It's quiet," Huck said and laid his head on his arm. "I don't see why my people have to chase you away. We could all live together and grow corn together."

Sparrow Hawk put his arm over his friend's shoulder, "They want to chase you away too. It's the traders. The men who care for nothing; who kill an animal with no prayer; who care nothing for the love of the people or the earth, for the children of tomorrow."

Huck said without turning, "I saw him in my mirror. It's Shut-One-Eye. He just ran down to that other field where the corn is spoiled. He thinks that's where we are going."

They both smiled, and mounted Treads-the-Earth who had been nibbling yellow daisies. The sweet corn was drying and whispered as the great ears shook like bells. "Hot diggety," Huck cried. "Look at that corn. Let old Colonel Davy put his eye on that. I feel a good song coming up now. We'll win the game this afternoon and then the Corn Dance with Black Hawk dancing. Let's make good medicine." He began, and like his dancing, his song always had a Yankee lilt to it and he often jigged like an Irishman making the Indians laugh lovingly. But now they sang together and the corn jogged dreamily and the grasses nodded and the squirrels chittered:

Let us dance the dance of corn
The peace of corn.
Ho! thunderbird go away.
Ho! Racing leave us, enemies run.

Ho! earth hear us.
The corn brings peace.
The corn brings peace.

⁝□⁝

They rode past Black Hawk's old field and there were the four Vandruff boys talking to their brother, Shut-One-Eye, who had just ridden up. They had been husking Black Hawk's corn. They began to shout bad words, laughing about the corn and making gestures that showed that the corn would not be eaten by hungry women and children, but would make the bad corn juice that made men mad or put them in a long sleep.

"Don't look," Huck said, "Make out you don't see them."

"Will they shoot us in the back?" Sparrow Hawk asked.

"They wouldn't dare, not this close to the Fort."

"I can hear the corn crying not to be made into the bad drink that puts men to sleep," Sparrow Hawk said.

"They're following us," Huck said. "Keep a stiff neck. We'll go by Colonel Davy's store." So they turned into the forest road that led past the store of the fat and jovial Colonel Davenport, where, today, after the corn-husking and before the winter snow, the traders, the mountain men, the voyageurs, the settlers would be gathered to tell tall tales to each other, and smoke and trade skins, and do their buying for the long winter months.

⁂

They rode into the clearing and they saw the Vandruff boys had followed them. In front of the store, trappers and traders had gathered and they all turned to see Treads-the-Earth with the two boys sitting sideways on her and the strings of braided corn hanging from her sides. Some of the men shouted out to Huck.

"How are ye, Huck? Who's yore friend? Still goin' round with that redskin?"

Both boys got off the horse. The Vandruff boys, their red heads alight in the sun like some evil birds, started to yell jokes and insults and some more men came out of the store to see the fun. Colonel Davy, fat and sweating with all the trade he had on this harvest day, came out and greeted them, "Why boys, glad to see you. How'd yore corn turn out? Yo shore have been slickin' through like water moccasins. Nobody seems to know how the corn came out."

The men began to laugh and the Vandruff boys to hoot, "Corn growers, eh? Corn growers, what kin you do with corn? Now if you had gold in that there poke you got there . . ."

Colonel Davy put his arms around them. "You bet

yore boots. We shore need corn. We need corn a sight worse than we need whiskey drinkers who set around all day and that's a fact."

The men were stilled and even the Vandruff boys stopped yelling, because Colonel Davy was a friend of President Jackson and of many white Generals. Colonel Davy waddled over and opened the green sheath of one cob of corn, "Why I never see such ears of corn in my life. Look at them ears. Look at the milk there." Some of the men came over and were astonished at the corn ears.

"Well I'll be dogged," Colonel Davy said. "You boys are aimin' to amount to somethin'. Now why don't you come and work in the store like I say. Get up in the world. What is it you want now?"

"We want land and corn," Huck said. "Land and corn, that's the only wealth for the red man and the white man."

"Land and corn," some of the men laughed. "Can you put land in yore pocket? Gold is what you want. I hear they're findin' gold out west now."

Some of the other men said seriously, "The boys are right. The red and white man ain't got no quarrel. Land and corn for all would settle a heap of trouble."

"Well," Colonel Davy said, "I never see the likes of this corn. And I shore aim to take an ear of it to President Jackson in the winter when I go to see him. I shore aim to do that and see his eyes pop out."

Huck said, "That sure is a prime idea, Colonel

Davy. Maybe we'll all get the same color eatin' corn. Maybe corn will make us brothers."

Some of the men laughed and the Vandruff boys had started a fight among themselves and two of them were rolling in the dirt and the others yelling. Some of the traders drifted over to see the fun.

The two boys mounted Treads-the-Earth and sitting sideways they rode away. None of the men were laughing now. Solemnly they watched the boys ride into the forest.

As they rode across the valley to Huck's place, the sun was again the sun of summer and there seemed to be no enemies among the leaves and they sang together their best corn song:

Grow peace upon the woman corn
Strong and tall
Grow peace
   The red, black, white, and yellow corn
Grows peace.

SONG OF
The Red and White Corn

Huck's father was chopping wood on the land he had cleared and planted. He was bent over like a jackknife, and was a thin Yankee, and he greeted Sparrow Hawk like his own son. "We been looking fer you boys. We thought somethin' happened to you for shore. But a bad penny always turns up," and he tousled Huck's hair. "You boys got to win that La Crosse game this afternoon. That Struts-by-Night stole some of my chickens last night. I got some plays figured out. That La Crosse is a game for a Yankee."

Huck's mother came out wiping her hands on her apron. "I'm mighty glad to see you boys. Those Vandruff boys when they get full of that firewater will stop at nothing. You boys wash up and come in and eat."

Sparrow Hawk always watched how Huck washed and tried to do the same. The mother kept on talking, "Come in and set. You been havin' too many thoughts like bees in a bee tree buzzing the senses out of you. You been thinkin' about crossin' that big river and never comin' back. I kin see the sadness in you and I know it fer my own. Ain't we been driv out'n Kentucky by the big title holders and then out of Illinois by the railroad land eaters? It's a sad thing workin' folks clearin' the land with their sweat and then the fat fellows comes along and takes it without a by yore leave!"

"Land o' Goshen," Huck's father said coming in with the corn, "Mama take a look at this sweet fat corn. You never laid eyes on the beat of it. Stick a tooth into that sweet kernel. Tender as a baby. Why I never saw the likes of it."

The two little brothers with freckles like Huck's, and dandelion tops, stopped eating buckwheat cakes to taste a kernel of the sweet corn. "Mighty pretty corn and our'n won't be ripe fer three weeks, and half that size and the nubbin half filled. Lookit how those kernels cover the cob to the tip, looks like Black Hawk muffled in his blanket. Why a field of them would triple the corn crop sure as I'm livin'."

"Wait till President Jackson hears about this corn," Huck said, "and he'll send out a man on a horse with a special decree to give the Sauks their land as long as water shall run and the grass is green."

"Well," Huck's mother said, "I hope they give us a decree for our land too. Yore father's got an order to move. One of them traders come out. Maybe they think there's lead on this land again. We been pushed west like the Indians, only difference we got the vote, and get more free land but we get the same grasshoppers, drought and speculators."

"The danged Governor of Illinois is out to get the Indians for the traders and the railroads. He was elected on a 'get the Indian' ticket and now he's out to deliver."

Sparrow Hawk could never understand the white men who elected their chief every four years good or bad. "We keep our good chiefs," he said "and when they are bad, look out for the women. They get angry and swarm like a hive of bees until he does better or is gone from our councils."

"Do yore women vote?" Huck's mother asked.

"Women are equal in our councils," Sparrow Hawk said.

"See there," she cried accusingly. "You see, for shame. Indian women vote . . . and you not wanting women to vote! Eat. Eat!" she said.

"I cannot eat," Sparrow Hawk said. "As long as Black Hawk is fasting and waiting for the vision so the people will follow him in what he has to do."

Huck's mother snorted, "Well getting three Indians drunk and having them sign a paper and then calling it a treaty why it's worse than the mortgage your grandfather signed in Kentucky."

"Now, mama," Huck's father said. "Don't get excited. They haven't brought all the soldiers yet from down river. General Gaines hasn't come to the Fort. Next month the Indians will be going to their winter camp. A lot can happen. Colonel Davy loves corn and lots of it to fatten the hogs, and it will make him so jolly he'll go to Washington before the heavy snow or just after."

"Now," Huck's mother said, "I tell you what you do. You divide that corn. You leave some here; we'll bury it in the root cellar. You leave some in your own mother's cache and you leave some in the cave below the Fort. One of the caches is bound to be there next year and then you'll see everything will be different."

"Next year," sounded sweet to Sparrow Hawk, like honey on a wasp sting, for it meant the elm bark lodges of Saukenuk and the wood smoke would rise again in the spring and the elms put out their green, and the pastures sweet again to the mouths of the ponies; it meant the sweet corn would be planted again in the old corn hills of their ancestors, and it would grow tall and sweet, full in the ear, milk in the kernel, and peace would live again for another hundred years at Saukenuk. Going back with Huck for the game of La Crosse they sang a good song, sweet as corn:

We strike for life.
He am I who brings corn to the people
Red and white, black and yellow.
Corn for the people.
Sweet corn.

Ancient Saukenuk

SPARROW HAWK and Huck sat in front of the lodge mending their La Crosse sticks. They could see the boys gathering on the square for the game. Soldiers were coming from across the island too but there was no sign of Black Hawk yet.

"In the winter lodge," said Sparrow Hawk, mending the deerskin sack at the end of the stick in which the ball is caught, "I am going to catch beavers and sell them and buy some land that has a paper saying it is mine. Why does the white man want so much beaver?"

"In the courts of the King of France, across the ocean, women wear beaver dresses with trains as long as a buffalo. Great men wear beaver hats six hands high." Huck grinned.

"White man is a wonder. Once Black Hawk told me he scalped a hunter and his whole hair came off in his hand—not real, and his head was shiny as a squash. A warrior told me once a man took off his leg in a battle and threw it. It was made of wood. At the Fort there is a man who takes out his eye and shines it on his pants leg." Both boys laughed.

Huck said, "And now we make corn that didn't exist before. There is a fire boat that walks on the water steaming like a serpent."

Struts-by-Night and Shut-One Eye were coming up the street towards them. They had their gambling bones in their hands and Sparrow Hawk saw with envy how tall they were, and Struts-by-Night was getting a little fat from the white man's food, from the corn drink too, and from sleeping too late and not caring for the needs of his people. But he had fine cheeks and black hair that made the girls all look at him twice.

"So you're fixing your La Crosse sticks. You might as well sleep the afternoon away. Your medicine is bad without Black Hawk." Struts-by-Night was picking his teeth with a long knife. Huck took his belt knife and began to throw it in the air catching it by the handle. "Black Hawk's run away. The whole nation will follow my father Keokuk."

"You want to bet that knife there that we'll beat you?" Huck said. "That's a pretty prime knife. You did a lot of spyin' fer that knife."

"I got a fine skin says we'll win."

"No, the knife."

Sparrow Hawk and Huck both stood shoulder to shoulder playing with their knives.

"Leave 'em alone," Shut-One-Eye said. "Baby angels that's what they are. Let 'em be. Le's go back to our game." They both gave a bad laugh and the boys watched them until they squatted down and began to guess which hand the bone was in.

Evening Star, who had been listening, came to the lodge door. "The sound of them and the sight of them is bad medicine. Has Black Hawk returned?" She looked up at the square where the players and the spectators for the La Crosse game were gathering and the drums had already started.

"No eye has seen Black Hawk," Sparrow Hawk said.

"Let him have a vision," she cried. "We cannot leave the graves of our dead, and the corn hills that, like mothers, have fed us. The Manitou will open the blanket of his lodge and let us see his face." The young girls went by and the fires burnt before each lodge making the corn kettles hum for the evening feast. "Keokuk will be here in all his baubles to persuade the braves to leave the village forever. Mend your La Crosse sticks well and win. The busy hands mend the heart." She went back inside cutting the squashes to hang for drying, then she began to sing a long song about the corn, and the sadness of leaving. "No more—no more," the song said. "This time next year we will be gone and the sun and the meadow lark and the hawk and the honeybee gone to us, rocked in the misted cradle in which the Old-Lady-Who-Never-Dies rocks the corn child."

Then the song brightened, and it was a day in the flower moon, when the mist lifts and the thunderbird comes. The rains and thunder and lightning beat the earth down, and shake the ground, and then at dawn the rain stops; it is very still, and a woman looks out of her elm lodge and she knows it is the day for planting corn.

Then the boys heard the song change and heard the sound of the women going to the fields, looking at the sky, for if you see eleven geese on corn planting day you know that the Old-Lady-Who-Never-Dies will give you a good corn crop. When the old corn hills are opened by the stooping women with their stone hoes, the smell of the cave earth is good and rich, the song said. The women sing into the earth and comb its hair fine and then drop the red and yellow and black and white seeds in, four to a hill.

The song told how the nights of summer then grow warm, and the first green spears show, and then the Sauk dance the corn-planting dance. The nights grow hotter and the corn spreads out in broad spears of green, crisp and fat, singing in the heat and the wind. The sun grows hotter and hotter, and the sheathed corn begins to show, and the antlers stand in the air. The dog star blazes, and the corn stands still in its bright warrior colors, and the woman's hair hangs from the green sheathed cob, leaning out from the towering stalks like women waiting for a

Song of the Women in the Fields

lover. And their lover is there, the boy pollen, shafted against the summer sky; on the still hot moon of August the marriage is made, and in the dark the corn maiden finds the bridegroom and a hush falls in the fields.

Then in the moon of harvest, the mother corn pours back into man, into beast, her riches, golden, pouring into the kettles, into the winter caches, into the pestle for grinding, into the corn cake, fattening the buckskin bags, making the heart content, for when the corn is good there is no fear.

Sparrow Hawk and Huck heard the song tell about the white and the Indian boy, who met for the first time and made the corn better and would now be in the story telling of the Sauk nation. It told how the Old-Lady-Who-Never-Dies was pleased and made a sign that corn should make hunger a thing not even remembered on the earth; for where there is no hunger there is no hate, and where there is no hate, no wars can be, so men lived as brothers. All a man had to do was open his mouth and the hot sweet corn filled and fattened him and all his children.

Sparrow Hawk rose and went into the lodge with his mother and put his hand on her shoulder and she drew his head towards her and he smelled the good odor of corn on her hands. He felt a bold song in him. "We will win La Crosse this afternoon. And that will be good medicine and bring Black Hawk down from the hills."

"Black Hawk will come," she said. "He has never left his people."

Huck and Sparrow Hawk felt good medicine now and they planned out a play between them that would be swift and set Struts-by-Night down on his haunches.

⁝▮⁝

They both felt fine now sitting in the sun working on their sticks, talking about their corn and their ways of winning, and they kept watching the trail for the tall, shrouded figure of Black Hawk. Suddenly the boys along the river began to shout, the women ran from their kettles, everyone from the square started to run and the boys ran to see what was happening.

It was the lead miners who went every spring up the river to the mines at Galena which the Sauk had mined for generations. They usually did not come back before the frost. Everyone was calling out loudly and the boys pushed through the crowd where the miners, men and women, leaned on their picks. "They beat us with sticks," one miner said. "They would not let us in our own lodges."

"But they have been our mines for hundreds of years," a woman cried out.

"They say we are taking *their* mines," the miners laughed a bitter laugh. They all sat around in the square to hear and a big old miner with huge hands told the story, how they had found their lodges full of white miners, and keel boatmen and ox-team drivers. Boats stood in the river taking out the lead, sending it down to

St. Louis, and ox teams left every hour of the day, loaded with lead, and men of all shapes and sizes were busy as beavers in the mines, and they all shouted at the Sauk in many kinds of language. "They are badgers and suckers," the old miner shouted. "It is our earth. I have gone down in that earth since I was a boy. It belongs to the great Manitou. Where is Black Hawk?" They all took up the cry.

"WHERE IS BLACK HAWK?"

"We should arm a war party and go back and claim our mines," a young warrior shouted.

Keokuk's son Struts-by-Night shouted out, "Fight now or follow Keokuk across the river and get what we can for our mines and our land from the white man."

The women cried out, "We cannot leave our dead and our corn lands and the lodges of our fathers."

"Call a council," some of the braves cried, "Get Black Hawk. Get out the war post. Black Hawk has never lost a battle."

Flaming Heart of the Eagle Totem called the men to council and the others withdrew and waited and Sparrow Hawk sat with his back to an old elm waiting. They knew he was the only one who could find Black Hawk and soon they called him. "I can go like smoke," he said. "No one must follow or spoil the vision," they said. "I will not spoil the vision," he said. "Then go," they said.

As he ran to his lodge he saw Struts-by-Night watching him and the Vandruff boys stood in a clot and his song told him—"Look out!" So he walked slowly and Huck whispered, "Squat down before your lodge, look like you're going nowhere. I'll get them in a game of bones. I'll bet my own knife. While we're playing, you go out the back way, disappear like smoke!"

So they squatted by the lodge with Evening Star crouching inside the lodge with her own knife drawn. The boys started to play. You held the bone in one hand concealed. You held out both hands, the other one bet on which hand it was in. If you bet the right one you won and got the bones. They shouted loudly and began to quarrel and sure enough the boys began to gather, Struts-by-Night with his jeering face, and the toothless Vandruff boys. Struts-by-Night pushed in. "You and your white friend ready to bet? You'll not have a feather left on your stick."

"Who speaks of white friends? Who drinks their white juice and has their dream of trinkets?" Sparrow Hawk said.

"Be careful of your talk, Sparrow Hawk." They all laughed their dog's laugh and passed a bottle around. Sparrow Hawk knew how hollow the legs become with the fire juice so he shouldered Struts-by-Night to start a ruckus and Huck pushed between them. "You want to let the bones say which?" Huck said.

"Sure," and all the dogs laughed.

They all squatted down, not noticing that Sparrow Hawk sank back into the lodge door and quick as a flash of fox he was out the back and up the trail, having left his jacket with his mother and heard her whispered words, "Go fleet, go strong and brave, my son," and in his moccasins and breechcloth he disappeared like smoke so she hardly saw him drift away into the September sun.

Sparrow Hawk drifted through the woods like a turning leaf. He could stand still as a tree trunk, sinking into the moss, into the life of the forest. He could skirt softly through the light without stirring animal or leaf.

Black Hawk was on the prayer trail and he must drift in like smoke and not scarify the vision. Soon Sparrow Hawk would be going on that trail for his first vision, after purifying prayers and sweat baths, he would go into the forest and Black Hawk would bring him water twice a day, and he would wait for the vision of animal, bird, or man which would then be his totem for life.

He sped past the signal tower and saw the guards and remembered when there was never a guard or a sentry at Saukenuk. He turned up the plateau of the Rock and into the forest and his blood sang with the keen scent and sounds he knew so well. The tribal life and mystery flowed in him like the river flowed in the earth, and he fled inside of everything the way Black Hawk had taught him, into the ways of every living thing, the bark of many different trees, the sound and substance of their leaves, and the smell, when you crushed them, of every plant and herb; the knowledge of the totem mark of every animal—the bushy tail of the squirrel, the stripes of the chipmunk—and he could tell every slight sign of their passing on leaf and root and twig and earth. He could tell who had passed, how long ago it was. Black Hawk had taught him to leap up with a weapon in his hand, as well as the steps of the Crane dance and the Totem festival and all the laws and ceremonies of an old and honorable nation.

As he fled along the forest he felt the strength of his father, and of all the great battles of his nation. The dark gathered at the base of the trees like a dark river. Slowly now, coming to the place of Black Hawk's vigil, he drifted forward like smoke in a dream, and he felt strong and silky and fleet.

He stopped, for he saw Black Hawk, and he knew he had come so quietly that the sharp small ears of the great Chief had not heard him and this made him proud.

He saw the small, fleet, strong body standing in the light facing the sun, which fell on his high-domed head, where all the hairs had been plucked in Sauk fashion, clear to the back leaving only the scalp lock. The long, sharp beak-like nose pointed to the earth and the high cheek bones lifted out of the brown skin that fit tightly over the whole strong body, hardened by fasting and long marches and many wars.

The air of the Good Spirit was around him, and he stood in the sharp, slanting river of light. The good song was all around him like the pollen on the corn; like the elegant quick legs of a grasshopper marked with black; or the perfect eye on a wing; or the masked stripes of a wildcat; of all that had rhythm and design. Sparrow Hawk stood a long time before he gave the whistle of the whippoorwill, and the high-domed head raised, and the ear turned slightly to test the sound and Black Hawk knew he had been found.

The boy stepped into view and the Chief raised his hand half between pleasure and displeasure, so Sparrow Hawk said quickly, "The council sent me," and he told what had happened. Black Hawk stood still for a long time, then the anguish broke in him as a dammed river breaks, suddenly torrential, and he spoke with that eloquence that moved them all.

"What can I do? No vision comes to me here. I see only the white soldiers—our own people spying out the land for them, stealers of our corn. I want no blood upon my land to stain the grass. I want it clear and pure and I wish it so that all who go among my people may find peace, and when they come and when they go out there shall be peace. These prairies belong to us. Look at me, look at the earth. We are old. The earth and I. We are old. The earth does not belong to us alone. When I received our earth it was in one piece. So I hold it. If the white man takes my country where can I go? Where can my people go? I cannot spare it and I love it very much."

Sparrow Hawk stood still, then he said, "The people wait for you Black Hawk. Tonight is the National Corn Dance. The warriors are torn between you and Keokuk. They have only to see you."

"How can I dance in the great dance when the Manitou has hidden his face from me?"

"It is more than the dance. The lead miners have been driven out. Even the women were beaten. The braves want to follow you to war. The men-with-hats, they say, must be stopped. They want to follow their leader who never lost a battle."

"They want to follow me?" Black Hawk stood before Sparrow Hawk.

"They want to follow you, Black Hawk, and Huck and I have harvested our new corn. The ears are muffled with kernels. Colonel Davy wants to take it to President Jackson. The good men-in-hats will see the corn and know the Sauks love the earth and want peace. The white man needs corn. The Great Spirit sat upon the earth and rested her hands and corn grew. Huck tells about how man made the corn have more kernels. Now the Indian who has kept maize like a baby in the cradle will give corn to the white man. You see that, Black Hawk?"

"I see it. I come here to find vision and you bring the vision from below. The white man has his vision too. Like your friend, Huck. Someday the two kinds of vision of the white and the red man will make a big dream. I will go with you. I will dance tonight. You will dance."

"But it is a night for braves," Sparrow Hawk felt glad and stood beside Black Hawk, close.

"There are many kinds of bravery and many enemies," Black Hawk said. "Some enemies have no scalp lock, and are not to be seen by the eye, and it takes courage to fight all of them. Come, son."

The two started down the forest path and Black Hawk, despite his many days fasting was fleet and no sound was made by them. Then Black Hawk who led, waited and let Sparrow Hawk take the trail. Then the song did hum in him like a bee; his whole being became sharp as an arrow edge, to sense every sign of leaf and hoof and wind, of weather, and of risk, to foresee every unknown barrier of twig and glide through as if in water. Though he did not hear a sound, he knew that, following him was the last of the great Sauk Chiefs, who had fought with Tecumseh in the Nations of the east and sat in the councils of his people.

They moved down and the sound of the Rock rapids moved up toward them and murmured like some ancient ghost of their tribe speaking of strength, of water and of day, of rock and time moving over man, wearing him to keenest edge of knowing.

Sparrow Hawk loped down the village street, trying not to show that Black Hawk was waiting on the bluff. He reported to the Council that Black Hawk would be there after he had rested. He loped past the big kettles bubbling for the feast, past the little boys dancing in circles imitating the braves who would dance their great war records that night. The Yellows and Whites were beginning to line up, some were warming up, throwing the tomahawk, bringing it back over the head, throwing it forward with shouts from both sides and the lines surging forward.

Sparrow Hawk belonged to the Whites. In the Sauk nation every mother at birth gave her child his birth color, either Yellow or White, and he always belonged to that team even when he grew up and went to war. It made manly rivalry and keenness.

Women were sweeping before their lodges with tree branch brooms, or throwing sweet grass into the fire to make a good odor. The young girls were combing and oiling their thick black hair, fixing their beaded dresses. Before each lodge hung the fresh corn, beans and squash, drying. Great mats of nuts and berries, cherries and plums were drying. Sparrow Hawk felt proud to know that on his mother's mats were the biggest ears of corn, the juiciest kernels, that would make corn for all, so there would be enough, with none fleeing like the fox, or shaking like the leaf for enemies, or hiding like the rabbit from the big guns.

In the lodges the braves prayed for grace in the dance and strength against enemies.

But there was evil in the day, and the eyes of the

women asked him, "Where is Black Hawk? Ask the White Father again. Let us stay on our land." Soon the crier would go through the village announcing to all the people that Black Hawk would dance and they would feel better.

Huck was waiting in the lodge and he had brought some ash and cedar boughs to hang in the lodge to dry for next year's arrows. It was good to think that next year the arrows would again be scraped round, with three grooves with feathers from hawks and he could make his own green from the corn color. The water drums began to beat from the square calling them to the La Crosse game.

Sparrow Hawk's mother made him eat a small bowl of corn which he held to the four corners of the wind. Huck did the same. Sparrow Hawk said, "Will your white god listen to my prayer, Huck? Is your god white?"

The big drums sounded for the game, a thrilling deep thrum that said, "Come, and may the best team win!" All the youths were running with their La Crosse sticks, with their little pockets of deerskin thong on the end, in which the ball must be plucked out of the air and carried through the goal. The youths, the yellow and white, with joking and bantering, were leaving their arrows, shirts, moccasins, robes and knives with the Chief of their birth color.

Sparrow Hawk and Huck were of the Whites and Keokuk's son and his fellows were of the Yellows, and

La Crosse

they lined up now against each other, some painted like the sunset, all naked except for their breechcloth. The most powerful ones held the middle ground. Huck was opposite the tall Struts-by-Night and Sparrow Hawk stood behind Huck.

They waited for the peace chief to bring the ball and name the number of times the ball must be taken by one side through the gates. The Yellows and the Whites faced each other. Then there was a commotion. Everyone turned and looked and through the elms strode Keokuk, dressed in many feathers and colors, his face painted red and black. He stepped beside his son with the Yellows. A shout went up from the Yellows and then the women began to sing and down the path towards the square strode Black Hawk, dressed in a fine robe and wearing a red coat. Some of the bluecoats clapped and the swelling of the women's song filled the square. He stood on the side of the Whites opposite Keokuk and called for the throwing of the ball. The prettiest young maiden ran forward with the ball and without stopping she dropped it between Keokuk and Black Hawk and ran fleetly back to the women.

Like a flash Keokuk had the ball in his ball stick and started for his goal but Black Hawk, lithe and strong and swift as a bird, seemed to pluck the ball from the pocket, whirled it swiftly, it flew into the air and was picked out by Sparrow Hawk who turned and gave it to the runner, Huck. But Struts-by-Night threw himself against Huck, knocking him down, so that the ball flew into the pocket of the Yellows and was carried swiftly through the goals for the first score.

The crowd shouted, and the players lined up again. This time Black Hawk again scooped the ball up but it flew into the air and was picked up by a Yellow, tossed to Keokuk who started toward the goal, but Sparrow Hawk leaped into the air, took the ball, and for a moment brown bodies collided amid shouts, and the ball spun in the air above them, all tripping and falling and running. If anyone was seen to touch the ball with foot or hands the referee stopped the game with a piercing whistle and the ball started in the center again.

The Yellows made three goals and the White made three and Huck winked at Sparrow Hawk for what they had counted on had happened. The easy life they led had made them winded now and Keokuk was panting from the white man's pork he ate. They were ready for their play. Black Hawk again got the ball, tossed it to Sparrow Hawk who pretended to run toward the goal with it, but he had really tossed the ball to Huck who pretended not to have it. While all the Yellows were after Sparrow Hawk, Huck, swinging his stick up with the precious ball, streaked away and then, when everyone saw too late that he had the ball, he had gone over the goal and won the game. A great roar went up. Even Black Hawk hardly knew what had happened and Keokuk and Struts-by-Night looked sheepish.

Keokuk, putting on his bright robe, said, laughing, "Well, you have won again, Black Hawk. But your winning is about over."

Black Hawk was putting on his red robe. "There is a saying that the earth does not hear one who will not fight the battles of his people." The Whites all picked up Huck and were throwing him into the air. "It's corn magic," Huck was yelling, his comic freckled face flushed. The Indian boys put their arms around the shoulders of the white boy and all laughing, they formed a circle. Huck drew Sparrow Hawk inside the circle and the drumming and dancing began—a circle of boys drumming with their feet, and going counterclockwise, a circle of girls all singing.

Flight and Struggle

After the ball game and before the evening dances, the village of Saukenuk seemed timeless and content, keyed to the harvest. They looked forward as they had for a hundred years to a pleasant journey to their hunting grounds, and their winter lodges, with the song of Saukenuk brightening the work of the hunt; the drying of the hides; the making of deerskin clothes for the children; and then the maple sugar making in the spring; and then the return home to Saukenuk to plant the corn. Their old immemorial journey.

"Tonight we will know," Sparrow Hawk said to his mother as they waited for the dancing drum and the ancient dusk crept among the tall elms.

"If Black Hawk puts up the war posts then every brave will have to choose. You are too young," Evening Star said.

"I have chosen," Sparrow Hawk said, "Black Hawk's trail is my own."

"Your trail is mine, my son," Evening Star said, and she laid out her deerskin dress, bright with beads and fragrant of the grass in which she kept it packed. "Has Keokuk come to the square yet?"

Sparrow Hawk laughed. "He will only come grandly after the fires are lit, like a turkey cock, with all his wives in traders' calico, grinning like geese. Where does he get so much silver and so many white man's medals?"

The drums began to quicken and the water drums began to speak as Evening Star put on her beaded blouse with her sign embroidered in quills—the sign of the Evening Star. She said, "I saw the Vandruff boys come into the square. They have big pockets in their coats and many bottles of the corn juice and they will try to arouse our braves for trouble."

The water drums quickened and the crier went through the streets calling them to come to the great square, rousing their memories. Evening Star's eyes were shining. The women loved the great harvest dances, seeing that the work was over for a spell and the crop good, and the corn caches filled for the hunger of their children. "Hurry, Hurry," she cried, "Don't forget now, son, tomorrow is the last day for gathering the swamp hickory so I can pound the paste and put the oil in the gourds for our winter flavoring. Hurry. Hurry, the drums call."

They moved out of the lodge into the bright stream

Portrait of Evening Star

of women and children moving toward the square. Sparrow Hawk felt the tall figure of Black Hawk moving beside him muffled like the corn, in his bright robes, his long hawk's face mysterious in the darkness. "Dance hard, Sparrow Hawk. Seek life from the Manitou with your feet. Do not think of anything for yourself as you dance but dance for life to exist in us, where your fathers lived and danced."

As they moved toward the square they saw all the old and young men of the nation with their totems, the crane, the hawk, the owl, the eagle, squatting in their headdresses and broad capes of feathers, and the people forming a great moving bright circle in the edge of the dark.

At a change in the drum one of the Chiefs ran forward with a burning stick and thrust it into the heap of brush. With a mighty crackling and roaring, the fire leaped like a thousand leopards into the square. The drums quickened and the people shone on the edge of light. Black Hawk stood as if upon the light, his hawk's face floating like a bird's.

Into the leaping light rode Keokuk, on a fine horse with its tail and mane braided in bright cloths of silk, its hoofs painted red, and the silver throat latch glistened with red and white bead work on Keokuk's coat and leggings. He sat stockily, but strong, on the white man's horse, his broad fleshy face painted red, and his hair drawn under a silk turban that spread out in eagle feathers at the back and he flourished his wampum stick with the scalps flying.

He dismounted and his braves took his horse. He greeted Black Hawk with his hand on his staff. He looked to Sparrow Hawk like a dandy as his braves all began a dance screaming sharply, "A i-eee Ai-eeee!"

"I hope you had a vision of peace and the way of the white man," Keokuk said in his voice used to filling the countryside with its oratory.

"Peace with honor," Black Hawk's face looked down like a hawk from a cliff eerie. "Peace in our ancient land, in our village, amidst our women and our corn."

"I hoped the Manitou would make you see the path I have chosen, across the great river into Ioway and not the path of the red coat."

"The path of the Sauks for hundreds of years has led to Saukenuk."

"The white man will give you much land and wealth."

"This is our mother the earth, the place that made you strong. Can you trade it for beads and drinks of Spirit water?" Black Hawk turned a piercing glance to the warriors behind Keokuk, "Would you give the bones of your fathers over to thieves?"

The women moaned like wind in the elms and Keokuk said, "They are many and we are few, they are a white river flowing from the east and you cannot stop them."

Black Hawk spoke in a clear voice that cut into every heart, "The history that we dance tonight was not made by that kind of speaking or from that bad heart. It was made by braves. These are the dances of my childhood and yours danced on this square where the Rock River falls into the father of waters. These rivers we remember as the great roads into our hunting grounds, into spirit and food, roads traveled by the Menominee, Winnebago, the Sauk. We remember the lodge, the meadow, the deep paths of the deer. We remember the river, and death is better than to forget these. May my arrow drop straight down from the bow if I forget my mother, my father, my son buried here. When the winter hunt is over we shall return, return to the old deep trails, home again. This is the path of honor and of courage."

The women answered with a high singing, the flutes and the gourds came into the drumming as the Chiefs went to their places and sat amid the robes and the headdresses and the brilliant regalia of their tradition. Keokuk stood, "Let our great warrior begin," he said, "Let Black Hawk begin."

But the braves of Keokuk, full of firewater shouted, "Keokuk! Keokuk!" The old chiefs shook their heads in anger at this impoliteness, but Black Hawk rose and said, "Let Keokuk begin and I will end." The loud drunken braves shouted, "Let Keokuk begin." He had risen in his robes and his vanity, unloosed his bright cloak, removed his leggings and stepped forward, his round, painted face cunning and cruel as Sparrow Hawk watched the dance tell of his first killing of a Sioux. He was fat and his story was all tarnished with his vanity. The women tittered behind their hands to see him strut and they whispered, "Why does he always go to the Fort first and pick out the best things for himself? . . . How does the white man's army know what we are doing?" Sparrow Hawk tried to watch the dance but he knew there was nothing in it to store away like in a hickory nut, for future use—nothing to practice by yourself to catch the grace and the strength, the wit and likeness of a good dance.

He finished with a big show of crossing the Ioway, of present history saying he was a great man with the whites and his own braves made a circle, making a cry, "Ha! Ha! Yah Ha!" But the people were restless, murmuring, breaking in groups, the medicine was not good.

The drums beat for other braves but everyone waited for Black Hawk. They wanted to be lifted into the courage, the luck, the good medicine. So the drums drummed Black Hawk and he rose, and the silence welded them all. The old Chief lit another pyre of wood, and the light leaped fresh upon Black Hawk as he removed his red coat, his leggings, and there was a sigh from all as he stood lean and strong, the taut muscles expanding on his lean ribs. He stood a moment, his body caught as a tomahawk before it is thrown, then he flew into space and took the center of a circle, raised his arms, rebuking the vanity of Keokuk, his song of self. He began to move into the dream. There was a stir as of a warm wind on water and they watched the thin hawk face, turning to shadow in the light, then burning alive as they were welded into the dream of Black Hawk, into the strength and rhythm as he told the story of each one of them, of the heart, of the courage of men long dead. The hearts of the young men were touched as by a feather of light. It was this way, he said, that courage was handed down in the Sauk Nation. It was all coming from him now, from Black Hawk in the middle of the circle. It was coming into him from the darkness and the fire and from hawks unseen in the sky, from Thunderbirds, from all the people in the darkness behind the firelight on the prairie. Black Hawk, everyone knew, was making beauty.

Even the young braves of Keokuk were silent, and in the shadow Keokuk was afraid.

Suddenly Black Hawk stopped, his face against the enemy, stopped in that moment of history when the people must stand against the river or go down. The people saw this, pressed against the danger a moment, then broke against it. The young braves surrounded Black Hawk crying the war cry:

Ha! ha! yah ha!
Ha! e yah! ha!
Ha yeh ha ha!

Black Hawk's Dance

Others had run to the council lodge and came back with the war post which they brought to the square and raised. It was their custom to declare their intention of war by throwing their war axes against it. The battered post stood in the square and the braves danced around it. There was a cry from the outside of the crowd and runners announced that a boat had drawn up to the shore from the Fort and Colonel Davy was coming up the path.

The women separated to let him through as he walked up, heavy of heel. He was scolding them. "Now what's happening here? Why wasn't I invited? I've been coming to your national dances for years and bringing many gifts. Now I am not invited. What's this—the war post? Now, now, what does that mean? Black Hawk! Keokuk!" He spoke as if they were little children and both Chiefs did not move.

"Has there been any violence?" Black Hawk said. "We are in our own village and do as we have done for a hundred years. My young men have become exuberant in the dance. The raising of the pole is only part of the national dance."

Keokuk stepped forward, "It is hardly that. Black Hawk here has moved his braves towards war."

The people made a sound like angry wasps.

"Now. Now." Colonel Davy danced like a fat goose in the firelight. "Now I know Black Hawk. He always keeps his promise. Why one winter I'd have starved to death and my family too if Black Hawk hadn't come through snowdrifts a mile high, and supplied the whole Fort with corn from his caches. Now I promised General Gaines there wouldn't be any trouble. Now you are going to your winter camp soon and I'm going to the Great Father in Washington and I'm going to take this new corn. Why he'll do anything for me—Old Hickory—we were at New Orleans together. . . . When he sees them ears! Old Hickory is a corn-fed, hog-eatin' man. Say now if you can grow more corn like I saw this morning, why say—I could raise some money in the East and buy this land—say, we could break the corn market, bust the corn market wide open, bust the East right open, send corn to Europe—open up the Mississippi to New Orleans —why, we could bust the East right open—build an empire right here . . . Now, say—there's an idea . . ."

The Indians did not move. Colonel Davy kept on with his goose dance—"Now just take it easy, go to your winter quarters. Wait."

Black Hawk wrapped his red coat around him. "We must come back to Saukenuk."

"Why shore you'll come back. We'll plant this new corn and we'll be as rich as Astor, won't we, boys?"

Sparrow Hawk spoke loudly, "We only want the land that belongs to us."

Huck stood beside him, "And I think the Indians should vote!"

Colonel Davy yelled, "Well, I'll be durned! I'll be hog-tied!" And he shook with laughter. The Indians did not laugh.

Black Hawk said to the laughing fat man, "In the spring we will come down the deer and buffalo paths of our fathers. We will come home again. Now we will go on with our national dance, danced for a hundred years at corn harvest. The young men will now dance, those who have killed their first bull buffalo."

Sparrow Hawk stepped forward for his first dance before the people of his nation.

HO!
The Thunder Am I!

THE MOON of the yellow leaves and the yellow grass had come, and all quiet waters had a thin skin of ice, while great birds were passing overhead, and the cranes were calling from the sky and sometimes they lit at Saukenuk for the last of the grasshoppers. Sparrow Hawk liked to watch as they stopped their feeding, lifted their heads and began to dance exactly as people do.

Everything seemed as usual when they were ready to go to their winter lodges unless you saw the children stop dead in their play when the bluecoats marched by or when their boats went silently down the river—or when Colonel Davy tried to make a joke and nobody laughed.

The moon of the corn was over, the last nuts and berries were dried, the oil poured into the gourds and the followers of Keokuk were prepared to leave the camp forever, and settle in the land of the Ioways. The followers of Black Hawk were going to their winter camp and would return to Saukenuk in peace in the spring.

Fires burned before the lodges. The women, their harvesting labors finished, visited in the square while the old men sat cross-legged and joked and looked sideways at the beauty of the women and told stories of great battles in the past. In the evening, in the smell of sweetly burning grass, the young warriors feasted on freshly boiled corn and there was drumming and dancing.

Sparrow Hawk and his mother watched the lodges where their friends would not return. At last the day came when they must depart, and some families were split, one following Keokuk, another Black Hawk, and there was the sound of parting songs, and sorrow.

The night before they were to leave, Sparrow Hawk lay in his mother's lodge, listening to the song of the tall elms he had heard since he was born, and the barking of dogs, seeing his father lying in the City of the Dead, Chippionoc, with all his weapons beside him, where his mother would spend the night weeping. Alone, he felt like making a prayer and he had risen and made a bowl of corn, and he held it to the east, and the west, the north and the south and he prayed:

Ho! you of the earth and the sun,
I wish to follow your course.
I am he, Sparrow Hawk.

Cause me to meet what is good
Ho! east wind like a young buffalo bull,
Very close do I stand to my grandfather,
Ho! I come. It is I, Sparrow Hawk
I wish to follow your course.

And he had slept and wakened to see his mother and the Indian women returning from the graves of their dead. He ran without eating, down to the river, and swam across to the island and around to the cave under the Fort, getting pleasure in looking up to see the blue-coated soldier above him. He did not like to go to the cave since the Good Spirit had gone, but he and Huck had put the third sack of corn there where no one could find it. It was dark and he found the corn and made a little Indian fire of crossed sticks for light and warmth, and said to himself—"Fire, I thank you for your light and warmth," and he sat reading the sounds outside the cave's mouth. Then he heard the soft sound of water like he had taught Huck to make, and in a moment Huck's wet head, like a beaver's, rose from the water and he pulled himself into the cave's mouth and the two boys squatted, Indian fashion together, and Huck was silent, having learned the way an Indian talks upon his thought and not before he gets it.

"Yes, you will come back," Huck said. "Do not be afraid. My father got a paper yesterday telling him to move, but he is not going to, he is going to wait to see you come back. Lots of the settlers are having to move. Scoundrels like Vandruff are in with the Governor and they make up titles that say they had the land before we did. Lots of settlers are moving anyway. My ma said she dreamed you came back in the spring with many pelts and maple sugar and that the corn grew so high you could climb right up to the sky on it."

"The corn," Sparrow Hawk said. "There is land and corn for everyone. I have seen the land empty waiting to be loved."

"We traveled days with our oxen and there was not a soul, but there are those who are greedy."

"And those who will not work together in peace with men of a different color," said Sparrow Hawk. "Though the Black Frock tells us all men are brothers."

"We have a prayer—it's called the Bill of Rights and then there is the Constitution—it says—all men are created equal and I will make my whole life to say that is so."

"Let us make a pact together," Sparrow Hawk said, "that we will stand together, the white and the red with the corn, as the corn has white, red, yellow and black kernels and the woman corn has hair of many colors, but all the corn says—let us grow tall with full ears and much fertility. Let us vow the heat of fire will make us stronger."

"Water will bring us together," vowed Huck.

"Earth shall be our mother and her paths lead us to peace," said Sparrow Hawk.

"And the rising sun will find us facing each other," said Huck, and they raised the buckskin bag of corn to the four directions of the compass. Sparrow took his knife and cut the skin of the fat part of the hand so their blood mingled, and they put the mingled blood on the buckskin bag that held the corn.

They lifted their hands together and after they had put the corn back in the rock niche, without a word, Sparrow Hawk marched to the cave mouth and sprang into the water and there was not a sound as Huck waited, then dived in, and swam to the island. Sparrow Hawk turned to see Huck make the shore just below the bluecoat who stood on the cliff, imagining that he saw everything. The two boys saluted each other in the morning of departure.

The day before going Struts-by-Night beckoned him up the trail away from the square.

"Sparrow Hawk, you're the straightest shooter we have and the swiftest runner."

"Praise from a forked tongue is as a snake bite," Sparrow Hawk said, folding his arms and looking down at the Rock River.

"I mean every word and if you know which side your moccasin is lined on you will listen to me. Tomorrow, bring your mother and the belongings of her lodge

Oath of the Corn Youths

and come to Ioway with Keokuk, my father, a greater warrior than Black Hawk and now he has signed the paper of the white man and he has all goods, all fattening things behind him. It will be food in your mother's kettle to follow us tomorrow."

"Yes, I see what your father Keokuk has beneath his fine robes and medals of the white man."

"What?" said the unwary Struts-by-Night.

"A stomach full of wind and lies."

Struts-by-Night's face seemed to turn black and he cursed. "Go and see—the white man will look at you from every tree, hound you in every ambush. You will die hunted like a rabbit."

"I will die for my land and my people, or Black Hawk will die, fighting hunger and the bad medicine between men." Sparrow Hawk walked away, his back prickling with the evil looks of Struts-by-Night, but he walked slowly, showing his contempt, hearing the shouted curses of Keokuk's son.

⁂

They broke camp on a morning when a thin ice lay on the river. They were late going. Keokuk would not promise to come back for the spring corn planting, or for Colonel Davy's visit to President Jackson. So the caravan started, women, children, walking girls with corn—the dog travois pulling the babies, and corn crocks, and the dried meat. They parted for the last time where the

Sparrow Hawk and Struts-by-Night

Ioway lay to the west, Black Hawk's followers going north along the Wisconsin, and Keokuk taking his braves with their families west into Ioway.

Sparrow Hawk rode beside Black Hawk on Treads-the-Earth. He felt proud when he lifted his hand, waving good-by to Huck, riding with Black Hawk, and he sat very straight so his fear wouldn't show. Now, this year, he must be the man of his lodge, shoot game, set his traps, see that his mother had as many skins as any of the women who had men and other sons. He had to step in the big footsteps of his dead father, and in the quick ones of Black Hawk. He looked at the lean face of Black Hawk and how the jaw set when they saw their nation split, half going one way, and half another. Black Hawk's sharp, long nose with the curving nostrils tightened as it always did, and his black hawk's eyes looked straight ahead into the ways of courage a man must go for his people and his nation.

He saw his mother with the women and children and felt how proud she was that he was now in the councils of Black Hawk and rode into the north for the hunting.

So they went to their winter lodge and it was a good winter for hunting. It was sad to split the nation and leave Keokuk and his followers, but Black Hawk's braves hunted with more zest to be rich for trading when they returned to Saukenuk in the spring. The families divided on the hunt and each chose their winter quarters and put up their lodges tight against winter, and the pelts piled up in the lodges.

Black Hawk hunted for all.

Sparrow Hawk hunted for his lodge and there was no grown man who had more pelts than the boy brought to his mother. He made the traps Huck had taught him to make. He also followed Black Hawk, afraid that Keokuk's men or the white men might kill him. His song was that winter bitter as the skunk cabbage that persists by putting its fountaining roots so deep and so far in the earth and heating itself under the snow so its green leaves come up in the whiteness. As he followed Black Hawk, unseen, using all his cunning to fool those ears, he would savagely sing in the winter winds:

I am a Sauk, I am Sparrow Hawk
I am he. I am of flint.
Let my enemies run like hares
Let my enemies shake like leaves
Let my enemies find a hole like the bear
Ye mountains tremble at my shout
I am a Sauk
I was born a Sauk
I die a Sauk.

He knew there were spies in the camp, sent by Keokuk to report to the white General who waited in St. Louis, saying he would get a militia and come after the Sauks. Then he knew one morning that his traps were being robbed. He found the foot of a fox and the fox gone. The next day he heard someone running ahead of him as he came to his beaver traps. So the next morning he got up very early and made the rounds of his traps. In one he found a fine white weasel and he tied it very tightly. Then he hid in the rushes behind a dead tree and waited. It was not long before he heard the sound of a white man coming through the swamp very boldly as if not expecting to be watched, and to his surprise he saw a familiar back go by him and lean over the trap and whistle softly at the fine fur caught there for which you could trade many things, and he put his arrow in his bow and then drawing a bead he said:

"Shut-One-Eye!" and Vandruff turned as if shot already, his hands up, both eyes wide open this time. His hands stole to his gun.

"Don't touch the gun," Sparrow Hawk said in that way that always frightened a white man, and it was surprising how he obeyed, especially if an arrow was pointed at him. "I've been wondering who robbed me. You owe me many furs besides other things. You are far from home. Perhaps you get a little for spying, too."

The Vandruff boy giggled and then he said cunningly, "I come to tell you yore friend Huck is dead."

Sparrow Hawk lowered the arrow and a blackness came over him.

"He was sick when I left and didn't nobody expect

him to live till spring. We look'n over fer yore corn and couldn't find hide nor hair of it. You wouldn't want to sell that corn, would you, now yore friend is gone."

Sparrow Hawk gave him a contemptuous look. "How many moons have you been gone?"

"About ten days, I think."

"You can have the white weasel, but don't touch the traps of the Sauk again. I'm going now," said Sparrow Hawk, "and I won't turn my back on you."

"If yore think'n o' goin' back to Saukietown, ain't no use. Some squatters tore down yore lodges and tooken everything, plowin' up yore corn fields like all get out, and they gonna stay, boy. If'n you was smart like Keokuk you'd have a good horse like him."

"You keep facing the swamp," Sparrow Hawk said, "and go back and leave the traps of the Sauks." He put the forest between them and turned running for the winter camp.

As Sparrow Hawk sat in the winter lodge, Black Hawk mused a long time, his keen hawk's face half hidden in his blanket. He had lit his pipe, held it to the four corners of the world, to the four winds, and he had let Sparrow Hawk lift it also four ways and take a whiff of the pipe of peace—"that gave you courage a man must have, even unto the death song, in the face of every enemy—seen and unseen," Black Hawk said.

Pipe of Saukenuk

Sparrow Hawk found it hard to sit as quiet as Black Hawk, but he held still until his legs had pins in them. He opened his mouth to speak, but the silence seemed like the stone cliffs on the Rock River at home. When he thought of this he felt an awful fear as he could see the eyes of his friend Huck and he seemed to be calling him, but he couldn't hear the words, and the bad eyes of Shut-One-Eye when he had told him his friend was dead.

Black Hawk then spoke about how they would have unity of all the Indian nations and then the White Father in Washington would see that they did not want war, but wanted to live in peace with the white man and raise the corn together. He said that in the spring, in the corn planting time, he would get Keokuk and persuade him, he would go to White Cloud in Prophetstown north in Illinois and they would join, they would get the Winnebagoes, the Chippewas, they would all stand together for the protection of their lodges and their corn lands.

Black Hawk, in the smoke of the fire, with the trees cracking outside with the cold, let his blanket fall, leaned toward the fire. "We must do all we can," he said. "That is all a man can do. To be brave is what makes a man—try to have a good horse and be in the front of the fighting . . . If you are lucky and count a coup or kill an enemy people will say you are a man—ride up close to your enemy. As you charge, say, I will be brave, I will not fear anything.

"Never tell a lie even for a joke. Do not say very

much, but listen. If you have a friend, cling close to him. Cling close to your people and their good. Think of your friend and your people before you think of yourself. . . . Cling close to your friend and your people and give your life for them."

This gave Sparrow Hawk courage. "To be a man, cling to your friend."

"Black Hawk," he said, rising, "I am going on a twenty-day journey."

Black Hawk looked up with his clear, black, distance-seeing eyes.

"Where to, Sparrow Hawk—where now in the dead of winter?"

"I go to set traps far," he said.

"Yes, that is far. Keep your eyes open under water, and report truly all you see."

Black Hawk knew he was not going to set traps, but he would wait to hear. . . .

"Ride close to the enemy," he said rising and putting an arm over his shoulder, "ride close to the enemy and, as you charge say, I will be brave, I will not fear anything."

Sparrow Hawk stood close to his near-father for a moment, then he said, "I will report truly as the earth speaks," meaning that the earth always spoke truly, that when a pumpkin seed is planted it is surely a pumpkin that comes up.

He set out, missing the moon of the winter storytelling, but he had no heart for it now, thinking his friend might be dead. Nights as he slept in the snow, he saw the freckled face of Huck looking at him in the eyes of beavers, and as he lay wrapped in his blanket among all the sleeping things in the earth, the bear, full of last year's honey, asleep, the curled snakes, the rabbit warrens, the little insects that would fly out at the first warmth, he hoped his friend was not sleeping in the earth, too.

He circled storms, enemies, and on the seventh day his feet quickened as they felt the valley of the Sauk and rose to the plateau above the Rock Rapids. It was further south and summer was on the way, but the water across from the island was still half frozen and the Great Manitou kept him on top of the ice and he felt it was a good omen.

The farmers would be in Colonel Davy's store and he wanted to find out about Huck. He went into the store and the customers turned to look at him. He thought how he must look for the first time, and the fire made his buckskin begin to steam, and his cheeks were on fire, he was so unused to warmth, but as he was about to leave, Colonel Davy shouted, "Sparrow Hawk. Well! Well! Well! You've come back to work in my store like I told you. Too bad about you and Huck."

Did that mean that Huck was dead? You could never tell with the white talk, but Colonel Davy went on measuring out sugar onto the scales. "I'm goin' to see Old Hickory now like I said, and you tell Black Hawk there mustn't be any incidents, not the slightest violence now while I'm there."

"Black Hawk has given his word," Sparrow Hawk said, and some men around the store laughed.

Colonel Davy pointed his pudgy finger at them. "Your word, gentlemen, ain't wuth nothin' and you ain't hardly wuth the powder and shot it would take to blow you up. You squatters ain't no prideful citizens. You come and work for me, boy, and you can make money and buy the things you want."

"I only want the land of my fathers," Sparrow Hawk said and walked out with the laughter following him like coyotes, and the little eyes watching, and the rancid smell of the white corn juice.

Then Huck was dead! But he would make sure, and he took to his heels through the woods, and knocked on the door before he could think, and Huck's father opened the door, and there was the good smell of their cooking, and the mother said, "Who's there?" and just then Huck himself stood, a foot higher and a foot skinnier, but alive and both boys began to ask questions at once, "What's the matter? Have you had the pox?" "What you back fer? Did they shoot Black Hawk like I heard 'em say they would at the store?" "Is the corn all right?"

"Hey wait, keep yore pants on, hold yore horses," Huck's father said. "You look bedraggled, my boy, take off yore coat and, Mama, dish him up some stew, he looks as lean as my old mule."

They talked and laughed and Huck's father said that they served another paper on him to get him off the land —maybe the railroads wanted it—you couldn't tell but he'd be danged if he'd be beat off the land again—he'd stay and fight along with the Indians!

Then Sparrow Hawk said he thought he'd go down to the village and they all looked at their plates. "I wouldn't go if I was you," Huck said. "They burned your mother's lodge."

Sparrow Hawk did not move, then he rose and said, "I'm going to Saukenuk."

"I'm goin' along," Huck said, putting down his fork.

"You know they call you something bad when you are with me."

"I know," Huck said, putting on his shoes. "But I'm a-goin'."

The two boys stood above Saukenuk and Sparrow Hawk thought this time he would cry. The great elms lay on the ground like wounded warriors, many lodges were in ashes and there was only space where his mother's lodge had been. Together they walked down the village street now strewn with refuse, and pale children who spit at them and called them names, and some men stopped sawing an elm and began laughing.

"They're only squatters," Huck said.

"What are squatters?"

"They are people who settle on the land with no

Lost Saukenuk

rights—no papers. They say they will plant corn in the spring and they are marking off the fences, those drunk fences as you call them—rail fences, they have guns so don't make a false move. They're also full of corn juice and have itchy fingers."

Sparrow Hawk stopped. From the birth lodge came smoke and the smell of corn likker. They were making it in the sacred birth lodges! Three men came towards them with pointed guns and one of them with jagged black teeth said, "Git off. Yore lookin' down the workin' end of a gun that means business. What you doin' with that Injun boy, Huck?"

"He's my friend," Huck said. "This is his village."

"Not now it ain't."

Sparrow Hawk said in Sauk, "This was the lodge of my mother."

"Talk United States. Whut'd he say, Huck?"

"He said he and the Sauks would return in the spring to plant their corn."

"That's what *he* thinks. Tell him to git."

Without a word Sparrow Hawk turned and walked back down the street with Huck following, past the great square, out of the village of Saukenuk, and he sang his flint song, for he felt that inside him some hard arrow formed and it was pointing and it was sharp:

Lo, the flint youth am I
I am he.

Now the zigzag lightning from me striking
Into the ground to hurl the foe
I am the flint youth
I am he.

Huck stood away, feeling afraid of his friend.

"The corn is still in the cave," he said.

"It is good," Sparrow Hawk said. "I will return and we will plant it in the earth."

And Sparrow Hawk went like the wind back to the winter camp of Black Hawk to tell him what he had seen.

⁂

Going north he fled back into the teeth of winter, but the flint song was in him. When he arrived, Black Hawk called the families together for a Council and when Sparrow Hawk told them that the lodges were burned his eyes avoided the eyes of his mother, so she knew and covered her face, and the other women began a sad sighing like the wind in the dying elms. Black Hawk said sternly: "Never before did we have an enemy that came while we were gone. Even enemies we have known have been those who do not come to destroy your lodges when you are not there, but to say, I am a man—you are a man—we'll fight as men. We have left our village without a guard for a hundred years."

The women came forward. "White families and their children live in our lodges? But how is that possible—do they not know we will return?"

Sparrow Hawk told them, "Squatters, they call them, just squat without papers." There was bitter laughter among the braves. "They are marking off the fields, cutting down the trees. They drove us off with guns, swearing a bad language. I looked at them and they did not touch me. They have poor muscles and they drink very much and have no good footing on the earth."

"Just the same," said one of the braves," a bear could slap you to death that has no teeth."

"Our lead mines, now our village," moaned the women.

Black Hawk said, "Tecumseh told me this, it is the same on every frontier. Stories and lies are told about us by the people who want our land, then the settlers who are with us at the first are turned against us and the army comes. It is always the same."

"Will we let them take our village then?" the young men asked. "Let us go back and burn their homes as they burned our lodges."

"If we do anything now an army of thousands will rise up like the leaves of this spring. It is true that Colonel Davy goes to see the White Father, let him go. He will take the corn with him and the great chief will see that we live in peace, that we plant the corn in weakness and it rises in strength. My people must do nothing so the finger can point and say—you are wrong. Now will I ask our British father to help us. I will go to the Winnebagoes and the Menominees. We will return to Saukenuk. Keokuk will change his mind and return in peace with us and we will have then twice as many men."

"The ice held me up, the winds brought me back," said Sparrow Hawk to his people, "my corn is good. The grass is coming through the snow. Come and drink says the water of the Rock. Come home, say the wounded elms, come home!"

So in one moon the water broke and said, "Come and drink me, ride me." They got in their canoes and went down the river towards the village of Keokuk. They moved into the south wind and the new buds opened every day into the moon of the flowers. The grasses were green for the winter-lean horses and the green juice ran down their whiskers. The skinned and cured meat was piled high in the canoes, great wealth for them all, and the shining pelts slowed their travel. They stopped for the maple sugar making but everyone was thinking of what Keokuk would say, and of seeing old friends.

In the evening their canoes were drawn into the shore of Keokuk's village and the women came running down to lift out the babies and the children and the old people. Great kettles were put on and a feast was made and they all honored Black Hawk and he spoke with his most eloquent tongue. Sparrow Hawk, sitting with the braves, thought never had there been such a speech spoken. Every heart was moved and there was warm agreement; the women looked tenderly at each other and the braves and warriors moved together strongly and the old men nodded in agreement.

Then Keokuk rose and leaned elegantly against his stick and gestured with round soft gestures and he said cunningly that he agreed with everything Black Hawk had said and it was good. Then he delivered a blow. "If you are willing to fight this mighty foe, this white army, then you must be willing to kill off all the old, the women and the children so you will be free to move over the earth rapidly, to fight them well. Do this and you can fight. Then you can engage them. For when one falls, a thousand leap into his footsteps. Do this and you will win."

The women moaned and the words of Black Hawk were as bitter smoke after the fire is gone, and they saw that there was truth in it. Black Hawk whitened and then he put out his hand and rested it on Sparrow Hawk's shoulder, and Sparrow Hawk stiffened and held his chief, strong as a young tree, unbending and full of the song of love and pride. The tribe split again and as the Sauks went to their canoes there was sadness and some of the braves of Black Hawk stood back ashamed but staying with Keokuk.

Sparrow Hawk helped Black Hawk to the canoe and they pushed off into the dark water, the sad singing of women on shore following them. In the darkness the young men who stayed haunted the empty places in the canoes and Black Hawk cried out in the darkness, "Instead of gaining strength we have now lost it, and we look now into our graves, and day and night the shadow falls across our face!"

DEATH

Let it Be Day

THE SAUKS broke camp when the spring sun was warm and the women standing in the lodge doors said it was time now to plant corn in Saukenuk. Evening Star said to Sparrow Hawk, "You killed your second buffalo bull in the snows of winter, my son, so now it is time you wore your father's deer suit." He put it on and saw with pride that he filled it out all over. He wished that Struts-by-Night would be at Saukenuk for he could look him straight in the eye now. He walked out where the women took down the lodges and packed the winter furs for travel.

Black Hawk stood watching the camp break up and the braves catch the horses for the journey. "It is good," Black Hawk said, as Sparrow Hawk stood beside him, "you wear your father's suit. Wear also his bravery. He thought not of himself but always of his people."

His old pony Treads-the-Earth nuzzled his hand. His secret wish he did not dare to name. In his father's deer suit how could he ride with the women? The braves were mounting the horses that were snorting and smelling the new grass pushing through the snow.

Black Hawk took the bridle of a new horse caught in battle that winter from their old enemies the Sioux. Black Hawk said, "Sparrow Hawk, Treads-the-Earth goes too slowly for one with his warrior father's suit, and the killer of the buffalo bull, and the warrior for our village in the coming year. So now you will mount Won-in-War and ride with the braves of your nation from this time forward."

Sparrow Hawk looked into the faces of the braves and back to the winter-thin face of Black Hawk smiling like a father, and now he saw with pride that he was tall as Black Hawk.

He became taller and pride filled his father's deerskin coat. "I will fight for the freedom of my people," he said. "I will watch day and night for the enemy. I will plant the corn of peace."

So it came about that Sparrow Hawk did not ride in his mother's canoe, or walk with the women and children any longer, but came back that last year to Saukenuk with banners, riding with the warriors on the bluff above the river, guarding the women in the loaded canoes below, as they brought their new children, furs, and courage back to Saukenuk. He rode on the plateau in the

Corn Youth Warrior

spring sun with three hundred warriors, all that were left to follow Black Hawk, but splendid and singing as they rode.

And Sparrow Hawk sang lustily:

Ho! you of the earth and the sun
I wish to follow your course
I am he, Sparrow Hawk
Wanting to meet what is good
Ho! east corn wind like a buffalo bull
Stand close to me as to my grandfather
Ho! I come. It is I, Sparrow Hawk.

So they came back to Saukenuk, singing and laden with the earth's bounty of the winter. Sparrow Hawk looked for Huck in the crowds of settlers and soldiers who stood silently and watched them pass, but he knew Huck would be at the cave and would know that they had returned, and he saw by the sun it was just the moment of the season to plant their new corn.

The riders did not stop but plunged their horses into the channel and rode to the mainland through the new green pastures. There they saw, in the ancient pastures of their tribe, the white man's oxen grazing. The warriors grew silent and rode into the village. They saw the corn hills plowed straight across with the white man's plow and the zigzag fences cutting up the fields. But when they entered the village the three hundred warriors grew silent and the squatters were silent, watching them. The elms no longer sheltered them. Some lay like old friends, prone and bleeding on the ground. Others were burnt and stripped. They saw where the lodges had been burned down and did not want to see the women's faces when they landed their canoes. Sparrow Hawk tried to keep his face like Black Hawk's, and not let the crying show. They had to guide their horses' feet away from the scattered bowls and kettles and the household goods that lay in the ashes.

Three men came out and stood with shot guns. One had a pipe and Sparrow Hawk thought for a moment he might offer tobacco and peace. Why could they not all live there? But he spat in the direction of Black Hawk and a child threw a stone which hit his horse and it reared so he leaned over and stroked its neck. "Kill them!" the warriors said in Sauk and Black Hawk raised his hand to stop the wasp rumble. "Not one move of violence."

"Don't get sassy," one of the squatters said.

Sparrow Hawk did not translate that, and he did not translate the oaths of another, but picked out some of the information for Black Hawk. "He says Colonel Davy has gone to Washington, has not returned. He says by the time he gets back all the corn will be planted. He says he would trade with you for furs and he has some good whiskey."

Black Hawk's stern face darkened. "Tell him I do not trade with whiskey traders," but his stentorian voice did not drown out the cries of the women who, with their children, now trailed from lodge to lodge, taking the empty ones, arranging to double up together. Black Hawk reared his horse and the warriors went on marking the land where they would plant corn. They met in Council that evening in the Square. Some things were the same: the birds coming north, the sound of the rapids of the Rock. The town crier went through the village telling what land there was to be planted, as the Council decided, and that the women would be guarded on the morrow when they planted. But there was not the joyous time when the land was given out to the newly married, or for the increase of a family, or for a brave deed. Now it was a question whether enough corn could be planted to ward off famine the following year, for corn was life and life was corn.

Sparrow Hawk saw his mother leave the lodge of Shining Arrow who had taken her in and he went to her. "The women go now to the graves," she said.

"Can't you wait till morning?" Sparrow Hawk said, thinking of the bluecoats.

"Your father waits my coming. He would be honored for your tears above his grave."

"Tomorrow I will go. Tonight we must see where to plant our good corn."

"I know," she said. "This is a home-coming I have never seen. So many guns."

"Yes, be careful. Five warriors go with you to guard. Stay close to them. Good night, my mother."

"My son."

Sparrow Hawk drifted off into the forest, making sure no one followed him, then he ran to the river, swam to the cave, feeling the cold water, and shaking himself like an animal. He knew someone was in the cave, so he stepped back and gave the whippoorwill call and it was answered with the mistakes that Huck always made, and the two rushed to each other in the dark.

"Huck!"

"Sparrow Hawk!"

They clapped each other on the back and squatted beside the little fire Huck had made. "I saw you ridin' in," Huck said. "Gee whillikers it was swell. Why you looked like something in a story book. It was wonderful. My ma cried like a heifer. I laid low. The squatter beat me up twict. And I want us to get our corn planted quick before they catch on."

"Where? The good ground we made last year is fenced off and plowed."

"I watched every move they made. I got a map here of five good places. We'll plant our prize corn in five places and one is bound to be saved."

"You should have been a Sauk," Sparrow Hawk said and they bent over the map, the black head and the shock of hay that was Huck's head, as he pointed out the five places for planting, the last one at Huck's own place and his father would plant it and nobody would know. There was a little island with good rich bottom land and that would be the next place and there were three others in the pasture.

"One of them is bound to be saved and we'll watch them all and control them and keep our records."

"The Indian doesn't know, like the whites, how to work with the Manitou. To help the mother earth do her work, to put it in a book! That would astonish the earth to be in a book!" Sparrow Hawk said.

"Tomorrow we will begin planting."

"You take the buckskin bag," Sparrow Hawk said. "The Vandruff boys have been looking for it and they're watching me."

"I brought a gunny sack to put it in so they'll think I only came to the store for vittles."

Silently under the noses of the bluecoat guards the boys swam down the night river with tomorrow's corn.

⁂

The next morning Sparrow Hawk was wakened by the sound of women weeping, and going to the lodge door he saw them talking to Black Hawk in the square and running towards them he heard them crying, "The grave ornaments of our dead are gone." His mother came running to him wringing her hands, "The grave ornaments of your father have been stolen!" "It's the squatters' children, they teach them nothing," another cried. "Now we will have to fight."

Sparrow Hawk saw Black Hawk's jaw tighten as he

lifted his hands for silence. "No," he said. "We will not fight—yet. We have come to our lands in peace and we will remain in peace. Today is the day for planting the corn and we will plant the corn!"

The women went away weeping but after they had eaten they came out of their lodges with the baskets of red and yellow and white corn; the warriors assigned went with them to the fields that had no fences, and the women began to work the corn hills. Sparrow Hawk went with his mother to comfort her and sat on the pasture grass. The sight of the women hoeing and stooping and bending and then dropping the kernels in the earth they had prepared, filled him with singing and his voice rose like the meadow larks' in the early sun:

The corn grows for us
The Sauk people
The corn makes many
kernels where there was only one
The corn grows for us
The ancient Sauk.

The women listened and then they took up the words. The corn grows for us. The whole field was singing and the women stooping and bending in the dance of the corn planting.

Sparrow Hawk sat on the platform beating a water drum and watching the sun rise higher and higher and dreaming of the corn this year which would be singing on the cob full and rich, when suddenly from the thicket bordering the cleared field Shut-One-Eye and four Vandruff boys, with yells and shouts ran into the field with white man's hoes and began to strike the women. Evening Star had worked far over in the field toward the thicket. Sparrow Hawk ran toward her where he saw Shut-One-Eye was beating her with the hoe. She was down on the ground and he saw blood on her bowed back. Yelling the Sauk cry of battle, Sparrow Hawk leaped upon him and they rolled in the earth. The field was alive with fighting and the running, screaming women. It was a sudden and short fight. Shut-One-Eye was too fat and his wind bad from drinking and smoking, so he did not last long without his long rifle to stand behind. He was pleading for mercy—"This is our land," he whined. "She's plantin' on our land."

"Yours?" the Sauk braves laughed. "Yours! The white man turns everything upside down. Turns his words, even our mother, the earth."

"Land can belong to no one," Sparrow Hawk said. "It belongs to the Great Spirit. Man tends it so he can live. We now plant corn for all here. Corn for life and not for your whiskey stills." Sparrow Hawk saw he was taller than any of the Vandruff boys as they ran them off the field and the women came back and Sparrow Hawk took his mother back to the camp to bind her wounds.

The next day Colonel Davy came back from Washington and the Council Chiefs went in the afternoon to the Fort, summoned there by General Gaines. The Indian runners brought back news that an army was forming in St. Louis, and Keokuk's spies watched everything the Sauks did, but the corn was up. Now they would hear what the White Father had said to Colonel Davy. But the presence of General Gaines made them afraid.

They met at the Fort and General Gaines said, "The boy may go."

Black Hawk said, "I have my adopted son close to me to tell you our plans and how we have tried to live in peace and plant our corn so we will not go hungry when the snow comes."

Sparrow Hawk translated this and Colonel Davy came in mopping his face and not looking them in the eye and he said, "Let the boy stay. He speaks the truth."

First Colonel Davenport looked at the floor and sweated very much and reported that President Jackson would do nothing. "He says to tell you you will have to go across the river and never return." To the question in Sparrow Hawk's eyes he said miserably, "Yes, I showed him the corn and he was interested. He kept some of it. I told him how you gave us corn and the army corn. I told him everything, but he just shouted to tell you, you must leave, that you signed the treaty, and you will get corn and the money and if you do not leave he will drive you out. That's what he said." Colonel Davy sat down in a kind of anguish when Sparrow Hawk had translated and before Black Hawk could answer, General Gaines, sitting at the big table with the white Chiefs said:

"I have come to carry out the orders of President Jackson. Either you go now or we drive you out dead or alive. Those are my orders. I want no boy with corn sent to dissuade me. This is the treaty the Sauks signed in St. Louis and do not tell me that three drunken Chiefs signed it who had no authority, that the land belongs to all of you. Do not tell me anything, but go, now!"

"We will starve if we do not harvest our corn first," Black Hawk began, ready to present his case but General Gaines stopped him.

"You will get corn," he said. Colonel Davy tried to say that most of the corn came from the Indians, even the settlers didn't raise enough yet, but before he could speak Black Hawk rose and drew his knife. The guards and the white Chiefs seemed too frightened to move. Sparrow Hawk watched him move swiftly to the table. General Gaines half rose thinking he was being attacked. Black Hawk threw the knife straight into the paper of the treaty. As it trembled in the paper he grasped the handle and tore the treaty both ways. "I do not know the lines on the talking paper," he said, "I set my name on none. The land is the land of my fathers and we will live or die upon it." Black Hawk walked out and Sparrow Hawk followed him.

In the next few days Sparrow Hawk went with Black Hawk to visit the farms, knocking at the doors to ask the whites not to sell the bad corn juice to the Indian braves. He translated about the corn and how bad it was to use the corn needed for food in the valley for this juice. Sparrow Hawk had to look away for he had seen Black Hawk's face in anger, seen it shut like a trap, seen it in grief and in joy, and in the dance, but never pleading. But he pled with the whites.

Some of the mothers looked very happy and asked them in for something called apple pie, and said their young men too fell down asleep with the bad juice and they were against it. Others said they wanted to trade with the Sauks and live in peace and some only laughed.

They came last to the Vandruff place on the island. Vandruff only laughed at them waving his long clay pipe and his fat cheeks coming up over his merry eyes, "All young people like the firewater made from the corn juice," he said.

Black Hawk stood in his blanket, "Our young people are not used to it. It gives them a bad spirit."

Vandruff laughed, "Good or bad, I'm going to sell it," he said.

Two days after that a young Sauk warrior, full of firewater was beaten to death.

That night a Council fire was built on the square and the Sauks met over the grave of their dead warrior. Across from Vandruff's island there came the sound of drunken singing and shouting. In the middle of their Council, some canoes landed, and three drunk young Indians with the Vandruff boys came into the council fire shouting and making jokes. Black Hawk rose and the drunk Indians fell back but the whites jeered and Black Hawk said, "Who will go with me? I want a party of five." He pointed to Sparrow Hawk to follow. In the dark, silently, they entered their canoes and still as fish they glided out into the water and landed on the island below Vandruff's, where the shouts and yells of the corn juice drinkers broke against the summer darkness. With their war axes the party swiftly crossed the island, pushed open the door to Vandruff's mill.

"There is one of your enemies," Black Hawk said, and pointed to the barrels of whiskey. The five braves, Black Hawk and Sparrow Hawk went through the party of card players, dancers and drinkers and lay their sharp axes into the barrels so the white liquid spurted out. Some of the most drunken ones tried to put their mouths to the spouts. Vandruff puffed up like a porcupine and tried to stop them but they pushed him aside and smashed every whiskey keg before they walked out, crossed the island, entered their canoes and went back to Saukenuk.

Black Hawk said to his waiting people, "We have struck at our enemy. Let us make a circle dance."

The shy young maidens moved out into the square and the boys joined them and they began the soft padding of the circle dance. It seemed to Sparrow Hawk that the circle of their arms could never be broken, nor their lives destroyed.

⁝■⁝

That summer Sparrow Hawk and Huck felt they were racing against time. He and Huck had planted five plots of corn and they tried to watch them all. Shut-One-Eye and the rest of the Vandruff boys, along with the soldiers at the Fort and their own kinsman, Struts-by-Night, led them a merry chase. One day in July when Huck and Sparrow Hawk fought five drunken soldiers who were cutting down the green corn with their swords, Struts-by-Night who had come back to hang around the Fort and spy upon his people, took the white man's oxen and plowed up another field of prize corn just ready to make the cob. The soldiers' horses were deliberately led into another plot of prize corn just as it was the tallest, the greenest.

"We've got two more," Huck said one day in August. "The plot in the river bottoms no one knows about and the one hidden in my father's patch."

The corn was forming now, the silken hairs fragrant, moving toward the milk, when Huck and Sparrow Hawk sat their ponies, looking in despair at the river bottom field where all the cobs had been torn from the stalks and fed to the horses. So now there was only the patch in Huck's father's field.

Some of the settlers moved away, tired of the fight between the traders and the Indians and the farmers. Huck's father got another notice to move, one of the traders claiming he had a deed to the land. But he refused to move until the corn harvest.

After his whiskey stills were destroyed Vandruff took a paper around to the settlers asking the troops to get the Governor to send the militia. Sparrow Hawk rode with Black Hawk up to Prophetstown in Illinois to talk to the tribes there and ask them for help should they have to fight.

For more soldiers came every day to the Fort.

They counted off the days for the corn to ripen.

But the Sauks would never see the wedding of the corn maiden again in Saukenuk, for one morning the Indian runners came back and told the Council that many men and horses were coming from the south and had camped the night before only eight miles below the Fort. They had killed a young Winnebago boy who had been attracted by the lights of the camp. They were not the regular bluecoats, but a militia recruited from old Indian fighters, backwoodsmen who were on an Indian hunt for the fun of it, to put notches in their guns. There were many and they hunted the Sauk as they would the buffalo.

There was no time for a Council as the next runners reported that the steamer of General Gaines had started up the Rock toward them and they heard the steamboat whistle.

Black Hawk spoke from the big square, "All go about your work as if you did not see the boat. Let the women cook, the men gather on the square, even the children play along the river. Nobody is to stop work or play. No one shall show fear. Not a warrior shall raise a weapon!"

Everyone obeyed. Sparrow Hawk gathered the children along the riverbank and they turned their backs to the oncoming steamer and played their games as if the guns were not pointed at them.

They all felt the guns at their backs as the boat came slowly into view with enough soldiers on it to blow them all away. Black Hawk sat in the square and turned his back to the river and said to Sparrow Hawk, "You tell me what is happening. I will play the white man's cards and they won't recognize me." He drew the blanket around him, laid out the cards, his hawk's face sharp and his eyes looking at Sparrow Hawk with a kind of laugh in them.

The river boat was named *Enterprise* and she came puffing into sight, black smoke belched from her.

"She is loaded with soldiers," Sparrow Hawk told Black Hawk, "and the big guns are pointed toward us."

Black Hawk laid down his cards, "Doesn't General

Gaines know he is headed toward the shallows. He will hang his boat up there."

"He does not stop. Now the soldiers are surprised that they see streets and houses. They do not know what to do. They have funny looks on their faces, seeing the terrible Indian, in the summer sun, living peacefully. Now the boat has struck. They have all fallen over each other." They both leaned over and silently laughed.

The boat had jarred on the shallows and the soldiers fell on each other like dolls. "Now," reported Sparrow Hawk, "the soldiers are in the water pushing the fire-boat. Now the General and his Chiefs are getting in a boat and coming ashore."

"They are coming to our village, then they will see that we want only peace. The white man walks so heavy, he will lose his teeth. I can feel General Gaines walking and it jars my back!" Again they both laughed silently. They could hear the Chiefs coming up the path towards the square. The party did not recognize them but passed on down the village street where the women at the kettles did not turn to look at them, and even the children gave never a glance at the stranded boat or the chiefs with their ribbons.

"Everyone is doing as you said," Sparrow Hawk said. Black Hawk's face lowered in a kind of sorrow, "The Sauks are a great people, honored in the island of the world. They are coming back now. We will play the cards."

The white men came back and stood talking near them. "A beautiful spot. Too good for them," said one.

"Try out some of your Sauk on these," another young brave laughed, and the first one spoke to Sparrow Hawk, in the foolish way white men spoke to Indians, "Fish much good here? Fish. Fish . . ." and he went through the motions of fishing. Sparrow Hawk drew into his blanket like an Indian pretending to be dumb, as if he did not understand. They all laughed.

"A stupid people," General Gaines said. "They deserve to lose this land."

"I don't know," said another looking back at the village. "This village shows a high order of civilization. I don't like to be here doing this. It's the Governor of Illinois with that mob at his heels. All the land speculators, racketeers, railroad land grabbers elected him and now he's got to deliver."

A horseman galloped up with a message for Gaines. "I'm from General Duncan of the militia. They are camped six miles from here and want to plan an attack tomorrow."

The group hurried off to the boat which had been freed from the shoals and was blowing its whistle, its black smoke in the air.

When Sparrow Hawk translated the message from General Duncan, Black Hawk threw off the blanket, rose, and called his people together.

Sparrow Hawk risked his life that night to go to the farm of Huck and whistle like the whippoorwill below Huck's window. Huck came out and he told Black Hawk's plan—to pack up the whole village and steal away in the night, go up stream so when the huntsmen came in the morning the village would be empty!

"Can you do that? Why it's in the middle of the night and it's going to rain. How can you take the women, the children, the old men and women and your horses?"

"Yes, we can do it, if the rain holds off till we make the rapids. The rafts are being made now and I must return. We must do it. These are not soldiers who come but killers and they will not only fight the braves but they will kill the helpless. We must slip away in front of their guns. We will get help from up river. They will see yet that we're only three hundred warriors and a handful of women and children. We steal away before them."

Huck's mother called from the doorway into the dark that held rain, "Huck—Huck—Oh, it's you." She made them come in, drawing all the curtains, and gave Sparrow Hawk hot soup. When she heard what they must do she cried, "You and your mother come and live with us."

Sparrow Hawk rose like a warrior. "I am a Sauk. I am totem head of my family since my father went to the Great Spirit. I cannot leave my people."

"Why they will kill you all!" she cried.

Sparrow Hawk said, "Would you leave your people? The books of Huck have told me how you became a nation, how you fought the enemies across the big water. You would not leave your people, each must stay with his own. Our Manitous are with us now, and with your prayer that Huck taught us—all men are created equal—"

"I'm proud of both of you," Huck's mother said, wiping her eyes with her apron.

"We take everything but the unripened corn."

Huck's father said, "Don't worry. They'll get this corn over my dead body. We'll harvest the corn here hidden in our own and save every kernel for you."

Huck's mother said, "Let Huck go with you a ways. A storm is coming. He can help your mother."

Huck began to roll some clothes together to carry on his back and he told Sparrow Hawk, "The soldiers and the General were asking me questions all afternoon and they asked me how would an Indian fight and I told him that Black Hawk would conceal himself on Big Island. He doesn't know there is deep water on one side between the island and Saukenuk. He knows only the other side where the water is shallow. I'd like to see them hunting you in that dense thick underbrush tomorrow."

"That is good," Sparrow Hawk said, "I will tell Black Hawk. They will be held up as they cross the island and maybe they will find the whiskey making of

Vandruff and they will never get to Saukenuk. We will be gone like smoke up the river. If we stay we die. If we go down the river we die. We will disappear like smoke and cross the big river in the north."

When the two boys stood in the door the rain had started and Huck's mother kissed Huck, and then she kissed Sparrow Hawk, who had never felt a kiss before, and asked Huck the word for it as they ran through the rain away from the warm light, where Huck's mother stood. Both boys thought the rain which now began to pour would cover their sounds and their going.

Even the worst enemies of the Indian will tell you that the withdrawal they made that night was one of the most remarkable in history. With the rain falling on their backs like knives, with the enemy stationed just across the river, with soldiers thick as lice, and guards patrolling the bluffs, and spies among them, all the goods, food, women and children, the old, the sick, the maimed were piled into rafts hastily made by lashing the canoes together. The ponies were silently brought under the noses of the guards from the plateau pastures.

Just before dawn they held the lashed canoes in the turbulent water. The night was black and the rain fell with a great sound. The men had to go and bring the weeping women from the graves at Chippionoc, and

Flight of the Sauk

Black Hawk and the warriors reared their horses in the rain.

The old men hobbled in the rain, mumbling advice. The young girls looked big-eyed from their shawls, helping the old and hobbling women. Some had to be carried. The children were wrapped and silent, taught never to cry in the night of flight. The youngest ones had their noses held so they would not make a sound. Even the dogs did not bark and the nervous horses reared silently as they were mounted by the warriors who would cover the flight of the women and children from the bank. Huck and Sparrow Hawk were to sit in the last canoe and cover the rear of the flight, while Black Hawk rode the land saying to all to give them courage:

"The trap is closing but we will be gone!"

The men, breathing hard, pushed the rafts, laden with women and children, into the dangerous churning water. Leaning against the oars, they turned the canoes up the Rock and they would be gone hours before the men stirred for the attack across Big Island.

Huck and Sparrow Hawk held their raft to the river, the white caps riding under them in the black wind. The great Thunderbird seemed to be over their heads blowing a dark wind, and hiding them and he felt a strong and terrible song in him as he felt the strength of his people and his own strength and he began to sing above the tempest:

Let us live!
Let us live!
HO!
Let us live!

And with each "Ho"—they bent to the paddle and sent the raft forward.

THE
Corn Youth Am I!

HUCK AND Sparrow Hawk were resting after counting what had been lost in the all night battle with the high river waves. They had gotten about ten miles from Saukenuk, pulled up their canoes in the driving rain, made lean-tos of boughs and skins, and were chewing some dried corn and sniffing the fragrant odor of smoke mingling with evergreen and the drying leather of their clothes. Little smudge fires went up from the lean-tos and some children and dogs whimpered in the cold rain.

All the warriors asked, "Are we on the war path yet? Or are we fleeing the enemy? Is the enemy following?" Sparrow Hawk and Huck asked themselves the same question that evening when Black Hawk sent them back to the edge of Saukenuk to see whether the enemy was following or not, and what had happened at Big Island the night of their flight. "I bet it was a sight," Huck said as they went silent as shadows back through the summer woods to Saukenuk, "I would of died laughing to see those soldiers beating the bushes for you Sauks and nothing but squirrels running out, thinking they were nuts!"

Sparrow Hawk grinned as they skirted a valley, carefully keeping to the ridges so they could look down on all their enemies. "I wish," said Sparrow Hawk, "we would meet Struts-by-Night and Shut-One-Eye right here! Now!"

"Boy," laughed Huck silently, "we'd really go at 'em . . . spies, and traitors."

They went single file silently. Huck, once in a while, snapped a twig that went off like a gun in the silence.

"It's too quiet," Huck mouthed silently.

Sparrow Hawk motioned that they make camp, wait, eat a little. They squatted in a ravine that rose back in the hills away from the river. They could see the river valley and the rock moving through the wet summer trees that hung sadly and silently. "Too quiet!" Sparrow Hawk thought, squatting there, and suddenly in this valley every bird and squirrel and tree and bush known to him became an enemy. It changed before his eyes and the long space of the valley became like a gun sight of the white man. The white man was taking the land and it was becoming different, the squirrels, the beavers, the buffalo were not as they had been—they were for the use of white men who made no prayers to them. He felt something bad was going to happen. He saw nothing.

Not a thing stirred. Even the animals had become enemies. Even perhaps Huck. He was afraid to look at him. He could hear him cutting some meat for their supper.

Now he was far from home and he felt his bones would not hold him up. There was an enemy that would follow them—follow them until not one Sauk remained. "Let's not stop here," Sparrow Hawk said and when Huck saw his face he wrapped up the meat again and they went toward Saukenuk as it grew darker and they skirted the little close hills. "Fresh horse tracks," Sparrow Hawk pointed. "A man stood here for a moment maybe looking at us. He has gone back."

"Maybe we can make my house," Huck whispered. Sparrow Hawk felt, not like a warrior, but like a frightened boy and later Huck told him that his face looked like one dead. He tried to sing his not afraid song. "Ho I am he, Sparrow Hawk!" but his lips would not move. He felt for the first time what it was to have an enemy behind every tree. But they could not turn back. He could never tell Black Hawk he had turned back and as they went forward each boy felt he had three heads, they looked in so many directions.

They went on through the river woods in the dark and the close trees were known to him, but now they would belong to the white man.

They would be cut down, the great trees, whose spirit was known to the Sauks. He felt misery in the wet night, the water dripped from the trees. He thought he had to see the corn in Huck's father's field. But every step he took turned his bones to water and set his heart thumping with misery. At last they reached the ridge that overlooked the joining of the Rock and the Mississippi River, where a thousand falls and rivulets murmured below them in the moist rich darkness of late summer. "You can smell the corn," Huck whispered. They pulled themselves over the old corn field . . . the corn that had been plowed up by Struts-by-Night.

Both boys lay exhausted and Sparrow Hawk dug his fingers in the old corn hills. The sky lay light to the horizon . . . and suddenly he heard Huck whispering. "There he is . . . someone is standing there."

Sparrow Hawk put his eye above the corn hill but could see nothing. Let us change places, Huck motioned.

Slowly, without a sound, Huck moved over and Sparrow Hawk lay down with his eye where Huck's had been and there he saw a tall standing figure rising above his eye, close to the ground. But it was not a man . . . the long, wet hair hung down and it stood dark and high above his eye and seemed to beckon. Then he saw the head nod. When he moved, it moved. Then he got used to the distance. He moved again and it moved. Then he laid his head down and began laughing in relief . . . laughing . . . his fever was gone.

"It's a corn plant," he whispered. "It has come up late from a seed fallen from the corn plowed under by

Struts-by-Night. It is a message," he said and crawled forward and digging deep he took the long moist roots of his friend, the corn. They put the long, spiral, green leaves in their hair, and ate the tiny half-formed cob, with the small delicious baby kernels. "Our mother, the corn," Sparrow Hawk said, "lives among the enemy and flourishes. So shall we."

They felt full of laughter, and brave and cheerful.

Before dawn they crept up to the island and saw General Gaines' soldiers quiet in their tents. The sentries had their backs to them. They stopped at Huck's house to tell his mother they were all right. They had pancakes, and Huck's father told them how the soldiers had been "flabbergasted," as he said, when they found the village of Saukenuk deserted entirely, the bird flown from the trap. They had to laugh to hear Huck's father tell it, as they all huddled around eating pancakes. "I was busting with laughter myself. The militia came up from the south rarin' to kill Indians," he said. "General Gaines came up the river on his steamboat and fired a few rounds into the brush, but then the militia swarmed in from the shallow side and he had to stop firing or kill his own men, and they beat the brush, yelling and shouting, and came out on the other side to the deep water. They came on Vandruff's cabin, and drank all the whiskey, and every man got lost from his company, and they were shoutin' and yellin' as they had to wait for boats to take them across. The leaders were quarrelin' whose fault it was, and by the time the boats come they was drunker'n a fiddler. A boo would have scared 'em stiffer."

Sparrow Hawk said solemnly, "General Gaines is a good chief and he must have been only training his men."

Huck's father laughed, "You sure got charity."

Then Huck's father sobered, "But the worst I got to tell you. They was so all danged mad they didn't find an Indian, and made a fool of theirselves, that when the boats came, they went to Saukenuk and burned it to the ground, every tree, lodge, dog, everything."

Sparrow Hawk was silent and the shadow of grief pulled his face into darkness. Sparrow Hawk could not speak for his heart was flooded with the dead life of Saukenuk, where they would never again celebrate the corn in the spring and the fall, where never would the young men prepare for the hunt and show their brave deeds in the dance, where time now would join the dead, and the great river pouring forever over the lost memories of Saukenuk.

Before dawn they told Huck's family good-bye.

"Remember," said Huck's mother, "we are white too. The traders and the soldiers are against us too. We need the same thing the Indians need, land and peace and corn. Remember that. We will struggle together."

And she kissed Sparrow Hawk the second time so he blushed but he liked it.

They left as silently as they had come. "Wish we could see," Huck said, "if our corn was still in the cave."

"It's still there. If this corn is destroyed we have last year's and we will start over."

The green sign of the corn nodded from their heads making them look from afar just like two corn stalks moving in the wind.

"People have brought the maize through thousands of years of wars, of oppression, always fighting to live . . . and we will fight . . ." Huck said.

"Yes," said Sparrow Hawk, looking at his friend, no longer afraid. When they got far enough away they sang their corn song fearlessly as the dawn came up and they saw far ahead the smoke of Black Hawk's camp, now the fleeing home of the last of the Sauks.

Lo, the corn youth are we
Huck and Hawk
The corn youth
Our enemies shake and hide
Lo we plant the corn.
We plant the corn.

Every day Black Hawk's caravan went further north, packing their robes, pots, axes, their bags of corn carried on the backs of women; the children sitting on the travois dragged by dogs; the older chiefs and medicine men, sitting the horses with their medicines and sacred objects hanging from their saddles. The young warriors went ahead to hunt for a camp and meat; and others brought up the rear to watch the enemy and see that no child strayed behind and to cover the path of their going so the enemy could not follow.

The rain alone seemed to follow, dank and miserable, but covering their tracks.

One night, as they lay in the rain, Huck said, "The worst thing, Sparrow Hawk, is that these are not soldiers following you, they are backwoodsmen, farmers with their own shotguns, Kentucky men who've been fightin' Indians right on into the west. You should see them. They're wearin' everything you can imagine. They're ridin' mules and old plow horses and they are out to get Indians. They aren't just driving you across the river; they are going to kill you."

Black Hawk walked back and forth one night when the rain stopped and the moon shone over the camp of fleeing Sauks. Black Hawk walked wrapped in his blanket so only his long sharp nose showed. Then he sat down beside the two boys and told them about when he was fighting with Tecumseh and he had heard about a man named Guy Fawkes.

Guy Fawkes who tried to blow up the Council lodge of the British King's city. Black Hawk had the idea of dynamiting the Fort, putting dynamite in the cave where the Good Spirit had fled, running a fuse up the cliff and blowing the Fort sky high.

"I am the only one beside Huck can swim under water to that cave, silent as a muskrat," Sparrow Hawk said.

"It is dangerous."

"A canoe can be seen by the guards. It needs a small quick one and I am the one."

"How do you happen to swim under water and know how to get to the cave?"

"Huck and I keep our sacred corn there all winter while we are in the Ioway camp. We met there."

"What a little fox."

"No I am a Sauk."

Black Hawk put his arm around Sparrow Hawk's shoulder, "We will yet make their relatives weep. We are Sauks, most favored of the Manitou."

This was one of the oldest of the war songs and Sparrow Hawk knew that soon he would be in a battle and could ride with the braves and dance the great National Dance.

"I will go too," Huck said. "I am becoming a fox also."

"Two foxes . . . our enemies call us foxes and we can become foxes. Why should you want to fight with us Huck, my son?" Black Hawk put one arm around each boy.

"My mother said our fight is the same," Huck said. "We need the same to live—land, peace, and corn . . . and both our nations will grow like the corn."

"Your mother is a wise woman," Black Hawk said.

"We will go when we see the sun," Sparrow Hawk said. "I will take my old pony Treads-the-Earth to carry the dynamite. We will wait in the canyon until night then we will go down to the Rock."

That night Sparrow Hawk made a dance that the young men attended and he sang and danced his dance of courage, and he got many followers to his dream so that many young warriors wanted to go with him. But it was decided the warriors should go ten miles and wait in case they would be needed. Sparrow Hawk and Huck were to go down with Treads-the-Earth and the dynamite by themselves and wait for the night.

Ten warriors rode with them and then waited on the hills while Treads-the-Earth led by Sparrow Hawk and Huck went on toward the Fort. They met no one. The soldiers were not following yet. "All the farm houses are empty," Sparrow Hawk said.

"Yes," said Huck ashamed.

"Have they run away from us?"

"Yes," said Huck. "It is because of the bad stories. When men are guilty they always tell bad stories about those they have wronged."

"They say we are ten thousand and we are less than a thousand. They say we take everything in the country-

Dance of the Corn Youth

side and Black Hawk won't even let us kill a chicken or milk a cow for our hunger."

"No one would believe that. The Governor of Illinois was elected by the traders and the traitors on a program of killing all the Indians."

"A bad Chief," Sparrow Hawk said. "I have seen him full of the firewater."

"Yes," said Huck. "He also tries to keep the farmers away from the prairies. He wants to leave it to the traders and the miners."

They lay all day above the Rock. Everything was still. Once a detail of soldiers went by below in the valley, hunting.

The boys watched them in a pine thicket. They watched the darkness come, the darkness that would cover them, and when it was deep as a robe Treads-the-Earth picked his way carefully, as if he knew he carried dynamite, and they went unmolested around the river to the cliff above the cave where the cache of corn was hid. They passed the sentry and could hear from the Fort the sound of music and laughter and dancing. They unstrapped the box of dynamite and let it down from the cliff side slowly, leaving a long fuse at the top. Then both boys swam noiselessly to the cave mouth, pulled the box down inside the cave when it was directly below the Fort.

"The great white bird who used to live here is gone,"

Sparrow Hawk said to himself. "Flown as we have flown." They found the cache of corn, the deerskin bag sealed with the blood of both of them. They held it above their heads and swam back. Before lighting the fuse they thought they would look in at the brightly lighted Fort. There seemed to be only the one sentry they had passed on the cliff edge. Everyone was merry-making, thinking that they had plenty of time to catch the Sauks.

They crept to the back window where they had often watched the soldiers dancing. Inside the bright light blinded them.

There was great merry-making and the fiddlers were outdoing themselves.

Huck whispered to Sparrow Hawk, "There are the settlers. They've all come to the Fort. They believe all the stories of terror in the country. To think that Black Hawk won't even let any of the braves take a chicken or a sack of corn. It makes me mad."

"Look," whispered Sparrow Hawk, and there, dancing with the General's daughter, was Keokuk, puffing and trying to keep in step, and red as a beet. And then they saw other of Keokuk's band dancing with the ladies, and they knew that Keokuk had joined the militia and was probably acting as its scout.

The boys had seen enough. They went back to the bluff edge and Sparrow Hawk said, "We cannot light the fuse. Black Hawk would never shed Sauk blood or the blood of women and children." They swam back to the cave, returned the bag of corn and threw the dynamite in the river and went back to camp.

The sky was clear and Black Hawk waited for them and his face fell when he heard. "You were right. The Great Manitou would close the door of his lodge if we killed women and children and the blood of our ancestors."

The next day the women packed everything again and they took the unmarked trail north. Their corn was getting low so they headed for Prophetstown where their relatives would help them.

Now the trails were not many for the Sauks. They could not go back and they could not stay where they were. So they must go on up the Rock to Prophetstown and get some corn, for their provisions were low. Black Hawk would let them take nothing from the countryside except the wild game.

At dawn the canoes shoved off into the clear water, and the morning sun. The warriors rode the plateaus and they were men now who had nothing to decide. Black Hawk rode before, with his red coat and blanket and his white horse, through the green of the forest. The others followed in their war clothes—the chiefs, the braves, the warriors in full paint, with all their feathers and weapons, and they sang and laughed, warmed in the morning sun and their decisions all made. Sparrow Hawk and Huck rode with them, keeping the canoes in sight. The women from the river began to sing because they knew the militia was far behind them and traveled with heavy wagons and oxen, and would be a long time catching up to them.

They were warmly greeted at Prophetstown and the kettles were put on the fire, and the hungry fed, and the wounds bound in herbs, and the sick children doctored, and the women began to sing again. Huck and Sparrow Hawk ate so much that they had to lie down on the ground and got so sleepy they could hardly listen to the Council of the Prophet. The Winnebagoes had sent their chiefs, also the Pottawatomies who had much corn land. But they were all afraid. The agents had warned them that whoever helped Black Hawk would be cut off from any aid. The traders said they would not trade with any tribe who aided Black Hawk. They said that it was a lie that the British father would help them against the American, even though the Sauks had fought with them in their wars.

They said that lies had been told of murder and pillage and the countryside was deserted, the settlers aroused by the false tales. Sparrow Hawk saw his Chief's face change from pride to astonishment, to grief that such tales would be told about his diminishing band of warriors and women and children and aged, who had touched nothing of the countryside in their flight toward the river and toward safety.

"Let the white friend tell us why they pursue us," the Prophet said, looking at Huck, and Huck rose awkward and shy and he said, "There are those who believe that anyone without a white skin must not be human. I am not one of those and there are many like me. Mostly those who believe so want your lands, and it is very convenient to believe that you are not as good as us then they can take your lands and feel good about it. Our prayer says that all men are created equal, and my grandfather died in a war to say that. Many of us are willing to die in any war to make the word true. Another thing is that to make you equal we should let you vote and then you would have a say, and a white chief like the one now in Illinois, put there by the railroads and the big traders who have made much money from your furs, and by the millers and others would not be in the white council to send soldiers to hunt you like rabbits. You should be able to vote or you are not part of the nation. You know that because even your women vote so that they are part of your nation."

There were murmurs among the chiefs of the wisdom of so young a one and then Black Hawk rose and said, "We must depart. We cannot stay and cause trouble to Prophetstown. And now it seems the other tribes will not join us. I was going to light the signal fires so that all our nations would stand together, but now I see that we cannot, so we must go on. Perhaps we can get some land to plant corn from the Pottawatomies." But the chiefs did not offer and Black Hawk said again, "We must go on. We must get across the Big River into safety. We are divided now and our courage wanes. My women and children are sickening. My warriors are deserting. I am tired and old. I have lost my first battle. They have burned Saukenuk. They have burned our young men inside with their firewater, destroying our best sons. They have turned up the bones of our ancestors on their plows. The honorable dream of the red man to preserve his nation within the new nation, the dream of Pontiac and Tecumseh, of the signal fires of all nations coming together and living in peace with the white nation to make a great nation is dead. Our signal fires are unlighted. We can only be Sauks and make our fathers proud as we continue to move away from the fight to peace. I am done."

Sparrow Hawk stood beside the aging warrior and the other chiefs of other tribes looked down into the earth in sorrow but they could do nothing. Black Hawk put out his shaking hand and rested it on Sparrow Hawk's shoulder and in every heart there was a sad song. How great a nation was the Sauk. What heroes, what braves came from the mothers. Now their day is done.

Then a commotion was heard outside the lodge and a runner came in crying that a great force of men now came up the river, seen from afar. There was confusion as the chiefs rose to leave and they were embarrassed, knowing that they did not want to be seen in council with Black Hawk. "We must leave and not be seen. The white men have not harmed us," they said.

"Not yet," said Black Hawk bitterly. "You still have your villages. Do not go. I will send Huck and Sparrow Hawk here with the white flag which I am told white men honor, and we will surrender and you will be safe—for awhile—until they want your land and your crops."

A white cloth was found and Huck put it on a stick and the two boys mounted their ponies and saw that the chiefs of neighboring tribes were leaving anyway with fear on their faces. As they left, the whole village watched Black Hawk pick five young men to follow them and report back what happened.

As the two boys drew near the camp they could hear the loudness of the white men a way off and the two approached boldly, Huck holding the white cloth on the stick. Sparrow Hawk felt every nerve in his body creep at moving so exposed into the white man's camp. It was against his wisdom and his nature, but he believed what Huck had said about the white cloth, and thought perhaps it had some honor in it, because it was white and not red or black. Danger—his body said, but he kept his eyes on Huck's confident face.

When the men who were eating looked up and saw

an Indian they went wild. The boys' ponies reared in the mad rush and Huck yelled, "We carry the white flag."

But pell-mell the mob came for Sparrow Hawk, crying, "Injun! Injun!" and they dragged them off their ponies and Huck kept shouting, "We come in peace. We come to surrender. Take us to the General." Some officers ran out of a big tent and tried to shout the men down but no attention was paid to them as the motley, undisciplined crew of backwoodsmen mauled Sparrow Hawk, and his whole being curled inside of him away from the rough hands. But he did not fight back, still believing in Huck's white cloth.

Then silhouetted on the bluff someone sighted the five warriors Black Hawk had sent to report. They had seen the seizure and were coming down the bluff side, and with a yell, the most aggressive mounted their horses. Without orders or order they took after the Indians who reared their horses, mounted the cliff again and led the militia away.

The ones left paid no attention to their officers and mauled Sparrow Hawk and even Huck, asking them questions. How many men in Black Hawk's camp? Where were they? Were they as fierce as reported? Sparrow Hawk pretended he did not understand their questions and Huck joked and gave them funny answers.

Then without warning a strange thing happened. Down the gorge, down from the cliff, from every direction, it seemed, the men who had chased Black Hawk's warriors rode yelling and cursing, back into camp. And the looks on their faces were so dreadful, their yells so blood curdling, as they cried that they had been attacked by a thousand warriors, and they were being pursued by demons, that the men in camp sprang from their eating to their horses, kettles were knocked over, the tents trampled and they screamed and yelled, "Black Hawk and his army of thousands are after us. They're right behind us!"

Sparrow Hawk thought—fear is a sickness terrifying as a silver snake. The two boys were forgotten as the men knocked each other down to get a horse or a mule. One officer whose horse was staked, jumped on, took off at full gallop, and when the tether tightened he flew over his horse's head into the air, and in confusion when he sat up, seeing the two boys, he fired point blank at them.

Sparrow Hawk had plunged toward the tethered and rearing horse, untied the halter and leaped to the unsaddled back. He took his ax and hurled it at the officer on the ground who had shot at him. He did not look but he knew he had killed his first man.

The free horse galloped with the running men and when he turned it at last and rode back for Huck, he was gone. He rode through the fleeing men and he could see nothing of him. Thinking Huck might have run to the trail he plunged against the flood of men and out to the creek but he could not find Huck. He went back but he was afraid he would be noticed as an Indian and it was clear to him Huck was not there. He had been shot by the bullet from the man on the ground and someone seeing he was white had taken him on the flight back. He could not follow. Perhaps he was dead.

There was nothing to do but go back to Black Hawk and he took the trail meeting an occasional soldier who did not recognize him but would shout,"Run! Run! They are coming after us!"

Sparrow Hawk rode fast thinking Huck might have stolen a horse, got back ahead of him. In camp the warriors were returning telling in amazement how they had led the white men on into ambush and then turned on them and how they had fled without a shot, as if they had seen ghosts and they ran so fast the braves could not catch them. "They're still running," Sparrow Hawk said. "Haven't you seen Huck?"

No one had seen him. "I must go back," he cried to Black Hawk. "Maybe he was wounded by the shot and crawled away to die. I must go back."

Black Hawk said, "We must bury our dead. We lost four warriors."

"I must go back," Sparrow Hawk said. "You must go too, there is much food there and ammunition. They ran from camp and left everything."

"We will bury our dead and return in the morning. When the white man runs away he does not come back for awhile," Black Hawk said. "You rest and then we will go. You look sick."

"I killed my first man," Sparrow Hawk said. "And it did not make me feel good."

"Be alone and sleep, then we will go for your friend, Huck," Black Hawk said. "You have done well."

"I have done badly," Sparrow Hawk said to himself, going to the lodge of his mother. "I was afraid as we rode into the white man's camp. I wanted to run. I was afraid when I leapt the back of the white man's horse and threw my ax and I did not look well enough for my friend, my good friend, my white friend, Huck. I have done badly." And he lay down and his mother asked no questions but covered him with a deerskin and he turned his face towards Saukenuk that was no more and wept:

Hold me earth, support me earth
If it is the day I die
Sky lift me up.
My people lift me up
Braid my horse's tail
Death,
Let it be day when you come.

It was dawn when they rode into the deserted cloth lodges of the militia. The ground was strewn with kegs, saddlebags, kettles, spoons, clothes. Sparrow Hawk did not look at the spot where the man he had thrown his ax toward lay. But there was no sign of Huck. No sign of struggle or blood, not even hoofmarks near the place where he had stood. There was no sign of him in the thickets or the creek bed.

"I think," Black Hawk said to the desolate face of his adopted son, "the white man must have lifted him on a fleeing horse and taken him back. He may be safe at home now."

"Or he may be dead," Sparrow Hawk said to himself, as they rode back dragging the food, the gunpowder, the guns on hastily made travois of branches and hides, and he rode, still looking in the thickets for Huck, still hoping by some miracle they would come upon him wounded, or he would ride out of the hills towards them, but no such thing happened and they rode into camp, the women and children running to see what food they had, chattering like magpies, happy to have something to put in the kettles.

He rode to his mother's lodge singing to himself the death song of Huck:

Let it be beautiful when you sing your last song
Let it be day.
If you would slay him O Shining One
Let it be day.

WE ARE
The Nation of the Sauk!

NOW THE SICK and hungry nation of the Sauk crept north ahead of the following enemy. The warriors grew restless as day by day they fled along the prairies, now emptied of farmers and settlers, as if they were an army of lepers.

Without Huck, Sparrow Hawk grew silent and grim. Now he had gotten used to hunger and learned from Black Hawk how to stand it. It was swift and heroic to fight, but this was a kind of battle Sparrow Hawk had never known. Where was the splendid battlefield with the braves shouting the Sauk war cry, and the horses thundering down the valley, and if you met death, it was in an instant, in the thick of battle, in a bright swift moment.

Day by day he helped his mother along the steep trail for they kept away from the valleys where they could be seen, and kept to the ridges and the steep banks where they could quickly hide if attacked. The food captured at Stillmans Run had long been gone, and Black Hawk still would not let them kill one chicken or steal the corn now ripening in the settlers' fields.

He watched his mother, weak from hunger, her feet bleeding from the stones, tear the bark from the elms, wade to her waist in the swamps for the calla lily or the jack-in-the-pulpit root which she fixed for the crying, hungry children.

Evening Star begged to be left on the trail with the aged who dropped out each day, but Sparrow Hawk said to her, "We must go on. We will be at the river soon. We will cross over! We will live!"

They left a terrible trail behind them as they went steadily west and north thinking to evade the following troops and cross the Mississippi into the Ioway country. They left a trail of stripped elms whose bark they ate; of goods and kettles left behind because the bearers were too thin and weak to carry them; of the bodies of the dead they could not stop to bury, which even the scent of the summer flowers could not hide.

The children laughed no longer but sickened, and many were gone and would never be warriors or young mothers singing the whippoorwill song in the spring chorus.

The old men crept along, weak from hunger and

Path of Broken Visions

some fell and never rose. Young mothers pulled their little ones along and they all made a moaning sound like a winter wind in summer, passing through the ripening harvest and never touching it. They were like ghosts. Sparrow Hawk forgot what a well fleshed person looked like.

But they all obeyed Black Hawk's words when he visited them at night, and they knew that every one of them was dear to him and he told them, "The gods do not know what fear is unless they see it on the face of mortals. Don't let them see it on yours." And they did not. Their faces rose and they plunged forward every morning moaning, "Let us get across the great river. Let us come to the great river now." And they went on day after day, losing count of the summer, passing corn that was not theirs.

Sparrow Hawk looked at the poor small ears and thought of the big fat and full ears he and Huck had made from their joint labor and knowledge, and now it would be lost, and Huck was lost and he sang his song of death that every Indian sings when the Great Slayer comes near in the wind. He sang as he felt his bones each day rise in him and he got brown and lean as Black Hawk, so they did indeed look like a black hawk and a sparrow hawk. Sparrow Hawk made a tune to the long march, to the bleeding feet, to the long flight they made of hundreds of miles, a flight remarkable in the annals of history for its military strategy, for the endurance of the people, for the courage and the bravery of a dying nation, the nation of the Sauk.

⁝▯⁝

The runners from the rear brought strange tales. General Atkinson hadn't gotten to Dixon's Ferry yet because his twenty baggage wagons, drawn by oxen, got bogged down in the sand and when they had to leave them the militia didn't want to leave the whiskey kegs full so they drank them empty and lay drunk for three days! So they were three days behind. Sparrow Hawk said, "I was always taught to follow the ways of the animal I was hunting. Imagine following us with heavy wagons and oxen!"

The runners said there were rumors that Black Hawk had an army of three thousand warriors, all with shining spears and gleaming swords and scalps on their belts, and that they looted the countryside and dashed out the brains of children on the trees. They said that the Generals boasted that they would bring Black Hawk back in chains.

They went steadily north and Sparrow Hawk slept with his face always toward Saukenuk, as they pressed ahead with no choice now except desperate flight, from the army that approached closer to their rear runners.

The traveling became more difficult, over rocky gullies and old rivers, and everyone tried to live and to press forward, and save their strength to cross the Mississippi whose current was strong and whose bosom was wide.

At night when they dropped from exhaustion a sound like that of crying birds went through their camp. Now they dropped in the meadows or in the woods, or even on a rocky hill and rested till morning. Sparrow Hawk had many dreams, some terrible, some good, of the old life and the years he and Huck were making their full corn ears, and the life of the ruined Saukenuk; and in his dreams it was whole and fair as before and the children were laughing in the dappled light that fell from the elms and the Rock Rapids made the song of water that was in all their dreams at Saukenuk.

Once he dreamed that the milky way was a sign like a rainbow in the sky, of the time when on all the earth there would be but one nation, and corn for all, and men of every color would live in peace, without want, without war.

Sometimes his mother had to shake him awake for his crying out in his sleep the name of Huck and she slept close to him always to wake him in the bad dreams. Now you would hardly have known Evening Star, but her luminous eyes still shone, and her black braids she wet and combed every day by some stream, and sometimes she stuck a flower there to cheer the others, as she would go among the sick and tell them she could smell the river, that they would cross soon and set up a good camp for their children and Colonel Davy would send corn, perhaps from their own corn plants which would soon be ripening in their ancient fields.

Then one day the runner from the rear said that a small party was coming fast and would soon be upon them, so Black Hawk with some warriors went out to engage them while the tribe went on, and evaded them. Sparrow Hawk was chosen to go and was given a task to perform, his first in battle. He was to ride ahead and meet the band of white soldiers, then turn and give his horse its head and lead them back to the ambush Black Hawk would prepare for them.

"Your first battle, my son," Evening Star said. "I would see you again but I would have you be brave and meet the enemy. I want you to grow to be a brave man, a good man. Think always of defending your people. Try to live bravely and well so that your people speak well of you and your memory is without shame."

"Yes, my mother," and she gave him the bow of his father which she had carried when other things had to be thrown away, and he took it and they looked in each other's eyes. Then he turned, mounted his pony as she watched him, and rode away, sitting in a different way than ever before, for now he entered his first battle. He had heard warriors say that everyone was afraid in their first battle, that the best warrior was most afraid and his fear made him a better warrior the next time. Black Hawk had gone to his first battle at fifteen. He had his father's

Warroad

bow in his hand and his own arrow made with his own cunning and the cunning of its flight would be his.

He was to ride back alone and Black Hawk watched him go, lifting his hand in salute, as Sparrow Hawk looked back at the sorry camp and he could see his mother lift her hand too as she walked among the sick and tended the hungry children. He saluted them and rode back to the enemy alone.

He was full of terror but it was a bright and terrible terror and it made a song in him, more terrible than his flint song:

Ho! the zigzag lightning am I
Sparrow Hawk
Striking my foes to the earth
Ho! the thunder am I
Striking terror in him
It is I, Sparrow Hawk!

He sat his horse in the summer sunshine, thin, burnt and singing loudly his lightning song, so the white warriors would see him and hear him singing. He rode through open, deserted meadows, down the roads, meeting no one. Around noon he saw them coming easily at a lope toward him down a country lane, and the summer day suddenly rose green all around him, because one bullet could take it away from him, and it was golden and warm, and he wanted to live. His heart was pounding bitterly in him and he gathered his breath in his thin, frightened ribs and sang out the Sauk war cry as loud as he could, and heard the birds whir away from him and saw the horses of the white men prick their ears forward. As he turned his horse in flight he shouted the war cry of Black Hawk, in his voice, so even a friend might have thought he was the Sauk chief, "Hi! yi! yi! Follow me. We are Sauks! Hi yi yi!" He did not wait, but let his fleet horse go and he could hear the hoofs of the white men's horses behind him, and strangely near him the caw of a crow, as he waited for the bullet that could find him.

Then he set his mind against being struck by any white man's bullet and lay flat against the speeding horse. He turned off the road and zigzagged like lightning among the hills, reading the signs of the earth as he went. The pursuing hoofs died down and he waited; he must lead them to the ambush of Black Hawk and not get caught or killed. When they lost him he shouted, "Hi! yi! yi!" and waited till he heard them and then flew on towards the ambush.

Black Hawk and the braves were waiting. He tore over the last meadow. He could see the thicket where the Sauks were, ahead of him, as out of woods behind him, came the white militia. For a moment he was exposed in the sunlight, and the bullets whizzed by him, but his good medicine held, and not one touched him. He rode straight through the thicket where he knew the Sauks waited behind the leaves. He doubled back but not before the militia entered the thicket, were taken by surprise, and those that did not fall turned back and fled across the meadow, pursued by the Sauks who chased them far enough behind their sick and starving caravan.

That night in the fire glow, Black Hawk told the remaining people of the nation of Sauk that the big river was near and he praised Sparrow Hawk. On a dead horse in the saddle bag that afternoon they had found a huge law book of a white Illinois lawyer who had come to shoot an Indian. To cheer the sick and the tired, Black Hawk pretended to put on spectacles, and opening the big book he imitated a white chief so well that even the women laughed. Black Hawk went to each one and peering down at the big book he pointed a bony finger at them and accused them of the crimes that the white man had done. "You stole my corn," he cried. "You beat my woman." For these things, he said, you did not have to be punished. You can use the forked word and the two-tongued justice will send you to heaven! In the darkness the bitter laughter sounded. Sparrow Hawk pretended to be the white Generals, holding a pouch before his empty stomach he strutted up and down comically shouting, "I will kill Black Hawk—when I catch him! I will certainly fight Black Hawk—but why are my men running in the opposite direction! We will catch up with Black Hawk tomorrow but my men are sleeping and I cannot waken them!"

That night they slept better for the laughter and the

next day the agony of the flight over the wild broken country lessened and they came out on a broad plateau, and ahead, below the thickets and ravines, there lay a mist. Sparrow Hawk had risen early, gone ahead, and he ran back shouting, "The river! The river!"

He ran to his mother who could not have walked another day, "Mother, rise up. It is the river. We will be across this day."

She tried to see but her great sunken eyes filled with tears, "Is it the great river? It is too late for me!"

"No, Mother, I will make a raft. I will run ahead and start making a tight raft and I will lay you on it and swim behind."

"The current of the great river is swift," she said.

"I too am swift. I will push the raft straight across and land on the other side so I can look straight back from where we started!"

"I once heard my mother sing a song about a river spirit who rose from the river and carried a maiden across. But I am old now. No spirit of the river will carry me across."

"I am that spirit," Sparrow Hawk said, "I will take you across. See how green it is on the other side."

"Oh my son," she said, "you are a brave man and warrior. How the great spirit of the Sauk lives in you. Your father lives and I will live—in you."

"You will live, Mother. The Sauks shall live."

The people were blindly running down the ravines

to the great river, falling face down and drinking, and putting their hands in it and some waded in and lay in the little summer waves that lapped the shore, and others put their children in, to heal their burning feet and their sore and hungry bodies.

Sparrow Hawk and Black Hawk stood at the river and watched what was left of the Sauk nation pour down the sandy ravine. "We are here," Black Hawk said. "We have come hundreds of miles to cross the river which we might have done at Saukenuk within a few miles, if the white man had not gone mad. Many have gone. Many have deserted me. But you have not deserted me."

"Would the moon desert the sun?" Sparrow Hawk said.

"My son," Black Hawk said, "now we must cross over. Now we must build rafts. The sun is bright. We will get warm and we will cross."

⁂

Forgotten was the weakness and the hunger as they all worked to make rafts of the willows. The first raft got to the current, whirled and sank, and the women swam to shore with their children, and started to make another. They must leave more of their goods behind, make the rafts light and lightly loaded.

Sparrow Hawk was everywhere encouraging the sick and the old, helping to launch the rafts. The next one was carefully loaded with three women and two old people and five children. The others did not stop to watch but working they watched. The women took it directly to the current on the broad blue river that looked so quiet but had such a fierce flow of water under it. The raft struck the current and wheeled, and the backs of the women bent and they held it, and with one effort sent it head on into the current. In the center the current took it about ten feet and Sparrow Hawk and his mother held their breath, but the women dug the paddles in, stopped and held and then plunged it another foot across the current. Now the river seemed to relent and took the raft, lifted it and threw it out of the current and the women swiftly rowed to the green shore opposite. There was not energy to halloo or shout, but everyone worked harder seeing that the rafts could make the current safely.

"Go on this raft," Sparrow Hawk begged his mother.

But she said, "No, I wait for you. The soldiers might be closer than you think."

"Our runners say they are a day behind us."

"Something may have happened to our runners, I will wait," she said, and too weak to help she lay against a piece of driftwood.

Sparrow Hawk had just launched the sixth raft, pushed it out where he had waded to his waist and he had been thinking, "This current would take us past Saukenuk," then he remembered that the village was burnt to the ground.

He was wading back when a black spout of smoke

rose around the bend and around the willows churned and puffed a steamboat. The Indians on shore stopped and held the gestures of their raft making in mid air as if they had been turned to stone. Sparrow Hawk stood in the water watching the boat come nearer, the guns pointing at them. It dropped anchor and it was so close he could see the bluecoats leaning over the rail and then he saw also Winnebagoes standing back a little as if ashamed.

Those on the boat were also paralyzed at coming upon the Indians so suddenly. The whole scene was quiet, even the birds, as the boat drifted towards them a little at anchor, and Sparrow Hawk thought comically, "How nice and fat they are," and realized it had been weeks since he had seen anyone but thin and starving people.

He regained his legs and ran toward Black Hawk who stood on the shore watching the boat, looking more like a valiant dead tree than a man. The warriors behind him moved uneasily towards their guns which they had left beside them in the sand, but Black Hawk stopped them with a slight gesture and he said to Sparrow Hawk, "Tell them we surrender. Tell them Black Hawk surrenders himself. Do not shoot."

Sparrow Hawk gathered his poor strength inside the cage of his ribs which he could feel sharp upon his breathing, and gathering himself like a bow, from his thin legs upon the earth he shouted into the day, into the summer air, "We surrender. Black Hawk surrenders." There was a moment when everything seemed to enlarge, the words fell across the water and the echo came strangely back, and then Sparrow Hawk saw the face of a Winnebago, lean from the boat rail in a kind of anguish of his own betrayal, as he yelled in Sauk, "Look out! They're going to shoot!" And almost at the same instant sound seemed to grow and explode in an awful light as the boat cannon shot straight upon the shore into the warriors, and women and children, and the animals shrieked from the thickets. Then the sand fell back and the water fled upon the shore as if to cover the crawling women and the crying children.

Those still alive ran back from shore to the thicket and the braves gathered around Black Hawk and took cover behind dead trees and fired upon the boat. The fire was answered by another volley from the big gun which raised the sand of the shore, and Sparrow Hawk saw when the smoke had cleared that his mother did not move behind the dead tree. He ran zigzagging through the sand and threw himself beside her, but she was still. When he stood the flint song came to him, like a pointed arrow inside him. Black Hawk stood beside him, his hand on his shoulder and he saw that the big boat had pulled anchor and turned and pulled away around the bend.

Black Hawk said, "They have gone to get more wood. Their leaving may also mean that the militia is

She Walks the Spirit-Path

coming over the hill by land. Our runners have been captured or killed."

"My mother is dead," Sparrow Hawk said, "and many are dead. Go back up the river, go up the Fox, hide so that the Sauk Nation will not die in you. I will stay and try to get those that are left across the river."

"I will lead them away," said Black Hawk. "I will go to the bluff and lead the militia back. It is me they want to shackle. I will lead them north while you and the braves get the rest across. Take the women across and guard them as you would the corn. A nation will live in its corn and women. Sparrow Hawk," he said, putting his hand on his shoulder, "you are a young warrior. I never saw a better."

"I have always in me the great Black Hawk of the Sauks," Sparrow Hawk said.

They stood facing each other for a moment. Then a runner came over the cliff crying that the militia was only a few paces on the plateau and Black Hawk ran for his horse and with the agility of a young man leapt upon it and drove the hungry horse straight up the bluff. The Sauk women began crying farewell to their Chief, and the braves stood straight and Black Hawk reared his horse at the top, turned and saluted his people. The faces of the white man's horses rose down the bluff, and Black Hawk reared his horse and led them away into the north.

The white militia thundered along the bluff and did

not fire one shot into the Sauks below for it was Black Hawk they wanted. For a while they heard the firing and then they did not hear it anymore, and Sparrow Hawk and the warriors began again to push the rafts into the water and load the women and children and now the wounded upon them. The dead they would have to leave now. Sparrow Hawk would have to leave his mother's body with only the white limbs of the dead oak to comfort her.

They worked hard and fast and they were just launching the last of the rafts loaded with the sick, the old and the women, ready to breast the river current when, to their horror, another force of bluecoats rode down the sand from the direction that the boat had taken. Women on the rafts, when they saw the bluecoats, tried to come back, some frantically bent to their oars to make the island that lay halfway across the river. The oncoming bluecoats shot directly into the scattered and fleeing women who held their children as they fell. The warriors ran forward crying, "We surrender," and the bluecoats shot directly at them. Women were swimming the river with their children on their backs, and Sparrow Hawk, shooting from behind the dead tree where his mother lay, saw some of them gain the island. Then he saw that the steamboat now came back around the bend, and drove into the rafts that bobbed wildly in the river, and then to his horror he saw that the men on the boat shot directly at the swimming women, picking them off as if they had been deer or buffalo.

The braves who had covered Black Hawk's run to above the Bad Ax River turned back. Sparrow Hawk saw them hesitate, turn, and he felt the flint form in his heart. He leapt from behind the tree, rushed upon the beach, no longer afraid, and he gave Black Hawk's cry as he picked up the red coat Black Hawk had dropped on the shore, and he put it on his shoulders, so they would all think he was Black Hawk. He gave his cry, so like him, even the warriors were moved to turn back. He cried the old cry, "Hold them. We are Sauks. Hi! yi! yi!" Some of the braves who had dug themselves into the sand cliff, came out with their muskets firing, and some stayed singing the death song of the Sauks from the hills, so it frightened the bluecoats and they turned to make the willow of the bend for shelter, and the warriors followed shouting, "Hi! yi! yi!" with Sparrow Hawk at the head in Black Hawk's red coat and with his cry on his lips.

Soldiers from the boat began to wade to shore, firing as they came and where one white man fell a dozen seemed to spring up. Sparrow Hawk crouched, firing, seeing the water of the river turn red and he thought, "The great river takes its children now at last, back to Saukenuk. Tonight they will be home in Saukenuk."

He felt the sting of the bullet when it struck him no more than a wasp sting, and he kept on firing until the loss of blood made him weak, then he took his father's bow and his own arrow and shot it where he was sitting and he sang his own death song:

Lo! Sparrow Hawk
He am I!
People of the Sauk
Behold me, stay with me
Earth stay with me!
But if thou would slay me
O Shining One,
Let it be day and facing my enemies.
When I sing my last song,
Let it be day with my enemies in front of me.
For lo! I am Sparrow Hawk,
He am I!

He thought of moving now into the great stream so the father river in the evening would deliver him to the white shores of Saukenuk, and he stood and moved toward it, but then darkness came over him and he knew no more.

Death Song of the Corn Youth

SONG OF *The Ancient Corn*

So Black Hawk lost his first battle, and fought his last one.

So ended a shameful part of the history of the times before men learned that they were brothers like the corn —the black, the yellow, the red and the white, alive and peaceful for summer suns, upon the green stalk of the earth.

Sparrow Hawk was not dead, only badly wounded, and he was captured that day and brought to Rock Island, back to Saukenuk which was no more. After days of delirium he opened his eyes, and who should be sitting beside him, offering him water, but his old friend, Huck, who also had been slightly wounded, and carried away from the battle that day by a fleeing white man who thought he was part of the militia. One day soon after, Black Hawk was brought into the Fort, unwounded, thin and unconquered. Some say that the Winnebagoes captured him up in the Dalles, in Wisconsin, but Black Hawk and Sparrow Hawk said always that Black Hawk gave himself up to the white man.

Black Hawk lived to be an old man on a farm the government gave him in Iowa. He traveled over America speaking to the white people to make them understand. He went to Washington and shook hands with President Jackson, who saw a man like himself, a warrior and a brave one, and Black Hawk said to Old Hickory, "I am a man and you are another." He also dictated a book and it was translated into English and he told how the Sauks had lived and loved and fought for their villages and their land. You can read now all Black Hawk had to say and he spoke so the earth could hear for he spoke much truth.

Sparrow Hawk did not know this but he felt it in his song—that there would come a time when the corn would grow big in the summers for all the children, of every color, who would play in peace together in the villages of the world and the earth would speak with her son, Man, in fruit and seed. He knew that the vision hunters can be shot by no bullet, conquered by no enemy, that they are the singing sons of earth, the Manitou loves.

So the story ends. The corn that was planted in the garden of Huck's father lived through that summer of the war, and the cobs were even more full of kernels, whole and fat and sweet as sugar. Huck and Sparrow

Hawk went on with their corn building, their work on the herbs and the seeds and the flowers, putting the white man's knowledge and the red man's knowledge together.

MERIDEL LE SUEUR was born in Murray, Iowa in 1900 and has spent most of her life in the Midwest. Her father was the first Socialist mayor of Minot, N.D.; her mother ran for Senator at age 70. After studying at the Academy of Dramatic Art in New York, the only job she could find was as a stunt artist in Hollywood. Her writing career began in 1928 when the populist and worker groups were re-emerging. While writing stories in the early thirties which gained her a national reputation, she reported on strikes, unemployment frays, breadlines, and the plight of farmers in the Midwest. She was on the staff of the *New Masses* and wrote for *The Daily Worker, The American Mercury, The Partisan Review, The Nation, Scribner's Magazine*, and other journals. Acclaimed as a major writer in the thirties, she was blacklisted during the McCarthy years as a radical from a family of radicals. Among her many published works are *North Star Country, Crusaders, Corn Village, Salute to Spring, Rites of Ancient Ripening, The Girl*, and *Ripening: Selected Work, 1927-1980*. The books for children by Le Sueur include *The Mound Builders, Conquistadores, The River Road: A Story of Abraham Lincoln, Chanticleer of Wilderness Road, Sparrow Hawk, Nancy Hanks of Wilderness Road*, and *Little Brother of the Wilderness: The Story of Johnny Appleseed*. She currently lives in Saint Paul, Minnesota.

VINE DELORIA, JR. is presently a Professor of Political Science at the University of Arizona. A former director of the National Congress of American Indians, he has published many books on the Indian political movements of recent times. Deloria is an enrolled member of the Standing Rock Sioux Tribe of North Dakota and is presently working on a book about Plains Indian religion and psychology.

ROBERT DESJARLAIT is a professional, self-taught artist from the Red Lake Chippewa reservation in northern Minnesota. His contemporary art, which is strongly rooted in the Ojibway traditions of his heritage, has appeared in inter-regional Native American art shows and exhibitions as well as in group and solo showings. He is a past winner at the Ojibwe Art Expo in drawing and traditional watercolor. He is listed in *Who's Who in American Art*. He currently lives in Brooklyn Park, Minnesota with his wife, Nanette, and their newly homeborn son, Miskwa-Mukwa (Red Bear).

This project is supported in part by a grant from the National Endowment for the Arts in Washington, D.C., a Federal agency.